ANNO
2020

JAMES MORCAN

ANNO 2020

Published by:

Sterling Gate Books
23 Whitsunday Key,
Papamoa 3118,
Bay of Plenty,
New Zealand
sterlinggatebooks@gmail.com

National Library of New Zealand publication data:

Morcan, James 1978-
Title: Anno 2020
Edition: First ed.
Format: Paperback
Publisher: Sterling Gate Books
ISBN: 978-0-473-74968-2

OTHER PUBLISHED BOOKS BY JAMES MORCAN (CO-WRITTEN WITH LANCE MORCAN)

The Orphan Trilogy

The Underground Knowledge Series

Debunking Holocaust Denial Theories
(with a foreword by Holocaust survivor Hetty E. Verolme)

The Heathrow Affair

White Spirit

The World Duology

The Me Too Girl

Into the Americas

Vaccine Science Revisited
(with a foreword by medical laboratory scientist Elísabet Norris)

Silent Fear

High Country Contract

The Dogon Initiative

PART ONE

CONNECTING

*"Life is what happens to us
while we are making other plans."*

–Allen Saunders

1

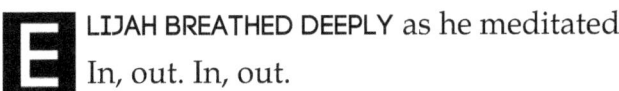

BALI, INDONESIA

ELIJAH BREATHED DEEPLY as he meditated.

In, out. In, out.

Even though his awareness was somewhere in the deepest recesses of his mind, Elijah was also conscious of more mundane things. For example, he could hear the palm trees swaying gently above his head in the sea breeze.

He could also hear the ocean waves. Not only that, he noticed how his breathing coincided perfectly with the waves breaking on the shore. Each inhalation ended with each wave's arrival while each exhalation precisely matched each receding wave.

These were the types of synchronicities Elijah looked for not only in his daily meditations, but also in his life in general. For him, they were mystical signs from the universe. And Elijah always paid attention to such signs as he believed in things like nature spirits, guardian angels and various other supernatural forces guiding humanity.

Guiding, if only humans would tune in and listen.

Elijah was meditating in the lotus position on Kuta Beach in Bali, Indonesia. The tropical body of water before him was part of the Indian Ocean. Known as a tourist mecca that attracted surfers and young partygoers from all over the world, the community on this day was like a ghost town. Even most of the Kuta locals were nowhere to be seen.

This never-before-seen state of affairs was a result of the international travel restrictions implemented by governments due to the Coronavirus, or COVID-19, pandemic. The virus had already infected several million people worldwide and reportedly killed a few hundred thousand, so authorities were taking no chances.

Elijah had been living in the coastal Balinese town since late 2019. He had stubbornly decided not to fly home to his native England when the virus had broken out in the Kuta district shortly after the New Year. Besides, the truth was he didn't really have a home. He had been a nomad for a number of years and there was nowhere his heart truly belonged.

He also believed in fate, so was not fearful about catching the virus. Instead, he felt that if it was his time to die, then he would die. If, instead, he was destined to live longer, then nothing would ever harm him including any virus.

I am a multidimensional, sovereign being, was his mantra.

At thirty five years old with a beard, dark, longish hair, and intense blue eyes, Elijah even had a devil-may-care look about him.

He placed his attention on the area inside his skull known as the midbrain. Having spent a year in the Himalayas studying under yogis and yoginis, he had learnt this traditional yogic meditation practice directly from them.

Meticulously following the steps of this ancient Indian method, Elijah breathed in specific rhythms in order to awaken the various glands and nerves inside his midbrain. According to yogic wisdom, fully activating these glands and nerves would eventually lead to enlightenment.

Elijah was not quite alone at that moment. Beyond the supernatural forces and beings he felt were surrounding him, he was also being viewed by a handful of people around the world.

The global observers were remotely viewing the Englishman's morning meditation via his cellphone that was neatly placed on a rock before him.

"Man," Elijah suddenly said, with his eyes still closed. "How did we get here?"

He took another deep breath, before he opened his eyes and looked directly into his phone's camera lens. He adjusted the phone's position on the rock in order to frame himself slightly better.

"And what the hell is this year all about?"

Elijah shook his head and smiled, before closing his eyes once more as if to intuitively seek answers.

After a few more deep inhalations and exhalations, he once more addressed those he was on the video conference with.

"Can there be a silver lining to all this madness?"

2

-.-. --- -. -. . -.-. - .. -. --.

WEST BANK, PALESTINE | RIO DE JANEIRO, BRAZIL

P USHING A SMALL trolley, Mariam walked alongside a concrete wall that separated her and her fellow Palestinians from Jerusalem. It was a twenty-nine-foot-high wall the 36-year-old had seen every year of her life.

It was also a wall she had seen some of her people shot dead in front of. Because of that and numerous other ghastly experiences it was a wall she hated with every inch of her being. For her it represented oppression, injustice, discrimination, humiliation and sheer terror.

On the other side of the wall was an Israeli military base that constantly monitored the Palestinian refugee camp which Mariam belonged to.

At least once a week, she had to walk alongside the border wall to the Israeli guard tower at the far end of the camp where she received water rations for her son and herself. Even though she and the camp's other refugees viewed the Israelis as occupiers of their land and therefore their oppressors, they were reliant on them for water among many other things. It was a complicated relationship to say the least.

The refugee camp was called Aida and it was in Palestine's infamous West Bank territory.

Ironically, Aida was located just over a mile north of Bethlehem – the historic town said to be the birthplace of Jesus Christ over 2,000 years earlier. Which was ironic as literally nothing about Aida was holy or sacred. In fact, to her eyes, it looked and felt like a scene from a nightmarish, dystopian hellscape unfit for any human being.

Mariam was one of around 800,000 or so displaced, UN-registered, Palestinian refugees living in the West Bank. Her parents had also spent all their lives as refugees in Aida. Before that, her grandparents had lived freely in the once thriving Arab village located in the land now called Israel.

That was until 1948 when Israeli military forces expelled them from that village. Mariam and all other Palestinian refugees referred to such expulsions and other ethnic cleansings of their forebears as the Nakba – meaning, "catastrophe" in Arabic.

Mariam stopped pushing the trolley for a moment and touched a small bronze crucifix attached to her necklace. A Christian Palestinian, she didn't know if she still had any actual faith left. Yet she liked having the crucifix on her for some reason. Maybe it was more that wearing her grandmother's crucifix somehow connected her to her ancestors' once free existence in the more fertile lands beyond the concrete wall.

As she pushed her rickety trolley further along the path toward the guard tower, Mariam looked around at the camp. She saw the dirty, littered streets, ramshackle refugee homes, and the *Free Palestine* murals graffitied on some parts of the ugly concrete wall. Taking it all in, she was amazed even after all these years that the world actually allowed people to live like this in 2020 AD.

What a ghetto I live in!

Aida was home to almost 6,000 refugees, about half of whom were children. They were all crammed into a tiny area well under one square mile.

Mariam could however recall as a little girl being able to move around more freely. For one fleeting moment her mind flashed back to those halcyon days as she continued walking.

Aida had been slightly more livable back then. The population was less and the camp's land size was larger. She recalled having more freedom and even remembered being allowed to regularly visit Rachel's Tomb – the burial place of the Biblical figure Rachel, at the entrance to Bethlehem.

Since then, former Palestinian leader Yasser Arafat had died and there had unfortunately been an increase in terrorist activities against Israel from some sections of the West Bank. This had led to tighter military controls being implemented by the Israeli army.

During that same time period, some of the camp's land had been annexed to make way for several large Israeli settlements. From that point on, the camp felt even more claustrophobic or prison-like.

Mariam and all of Aida's residents knew such Israeli settlements were illegal under international law. However, they were powerless to stop such human rights violations. Voicing disapproval was basically impossible given that many caught peacefully protesting in the camp had already earned themselves prison sentences.

As she reached the guard tower protruding from the wall, the face of a young Israeli soldier appeared through a peep hole in the heavily barricaded door.

He barked instructions in broken Arabic, telling her to approach slowly and show hands at all times. Mariam knew the drill although things had gotten more complex since the recent Coronavirus measures had been imposed. She donned her surgical face mask and antibacterial gloves before presenting her identification card as per usual.

Finally, when the young soldier was satisfied, he opened up the steel door, ventured out a few feet into the camp and gestured for Mariam to pull the plastic containers off the trolley she'd been pushing. As he began to fill up the containers, Mariam couldn't pull her eyes away from the big assault rifle he carried over his shoulder. She then studied his helmet and imposing body armor. The combined effect of all the military gear was it made the otherwise-angelic-looking soldier look tough – and frightening to a mere civilian.

Things had been even more tense than usual at the camp of late and Mariam could sense the soldier was on guard for anything untoward. He constantly scanned his surroundings to make sure no other refugees were in the vicinity.

Only the day before, the camp had been tear-gassed because some teenage Palestinian activists had thrown rocks and Molotov cocktails at the guard towers.

And in the last month alone, Mariam had experienced three traumatic events that she wished to forget like most of her other memories.

Firstly, she'd had a gun pointed between her eyes when she had tried to defend a six year old boy who soldiers were shouting at. Secondly, she had been woken at four o'clock in the morning when armed soldiers had broken into the camp and thrown deafening sound grenades. Thirdly, she had witnessed the brutal manhandling of a frail, elderly refugee who fell over and suffered a broken hip.

As the young soldier filled up the last of Mariam's water bottles, he sighed. Mariam knew that exact feeling, but unlike this Israeli she was clean out of sighs. She was out of tears, too, and just felt numb. She glanced up at the guard tower above them. It cast a long dark shadow, which seemed fitting somehow, and it truly was the most horrible piece of architecture she'd ever seen.

Once she had been allocated her water ration, Mariam began to wheel her trolley back toward her home. She went along the exact same route, following *The Wall*.

That evening, after returning to her apartment and feeding her thirteen year old son dinner, Mariam managed to get online.

Aida, like most of Palestine's West Bank, only had electricity about half of the time. This was mostly due to frequent, unscheduled power cuts. Lights were constantly flickering out, ovens went off in the middle of preparing meals, and computers often died before work could be saved.

Fortunately, Mariam's old computer was operating just fine so far this evening and she hoped the electricity would hold out for the task she needed to get out of the way.

Three days earlier, she had been surprised to see a friend request on her Goodreads social media account.

It was from: *Hanan*.

When she had first seen that name in her notifications it had immediately created a flashback to a life she'd long since forgotten, or at least suppressed in her mind.

In an accompanying Goodreads message, Hanan had requested a video chat. Mariam had reluctantly agreed to it but now she didn't even know why she had.

I have no future, Hanan, so why would I care for the past that brought me to this sad, helpless point?

Later that evening, Mariam and Hanan stared at each other via their computers' web-cams. Even though they had just engaged in some reasonably pleasant small talk, both women were tense and full of emotion. And they could both see that in each other's eyes.

Hanan, who was seated in her home office in her upmarket apartment in Rio de Janeiro, Brazil, was absentmindedly fiddling with a silver crucifix that hung from around her neck. She was also a Christian Palestinian. Not only that, but she was born in the West Bank and had as a younger women spent much time in the Aida Refugee Camp.

Hanan went to speak, but before she could get a word out, a door opened in Mariam's dingy apartment. A lot of commotion could be heard from Mariam's end all of a sudden.

"Sorry," a distracted Mariam uttered in Arabic to Hanan.

Hanan gestured to Mariam that everything was fine and that she should attend to whatever she needed to do.

Thirty-four-year-old Hanan waited patiently as Mariam vanished from her webcam's view. After a few minutes passed, she attended to some work at her desk while awaiting Mariam's return. An architect by profession, Hanan looked at some floor designs for a new hospital her company had been commissioned to assist with. The hospital, located near the Amazon jungle, was part of the Brazilian government's far-reaching plans to cope with the expected influx of infected COVID-19 citizens.

As Hanan worked, she could hear Mariam jabbering away to someone off-camera. Mariam was mentioning aspects of the health and safety measures for Coronavirus protocols, as well as the Palestinian Authority's rules regarding a lockdown.

Hanan could not see who Mariam was talking to, but by the caring tone in the Aida refugee's voice it was obvious she was advising a loved one.

Mariam and her son shared the small apartment with three other refugee families, so the noise in the house was almost constant.

Hanan could also hear what sounded like neighbors yelling at each other.

The Rio-based architect remembered this existence well. She was aware refugees in Aida were packed together so tightly in their little concrete homes that they could hear neighbors chopping up food for dinner, snoring or even having sex.

Finally, Mariam sat back down before her computer and looked on screen to discover Hanan was still there.

Having just dealt with some unexpected drama within her household, Mariam felt even less patient than before with Hanan. "So... I really don't want to open up old wounds here," Mariam said.

"That's not my intention, Mariam."

"Then what is your intention?"

"I don't know exactly." Hanan replied "It's just that... "

"Just that what?" Mariam asked tersely.

Hanan took a deep breath as she looked at the pained, stressed face of her fellow Palestinian. It was a face that was once so beautiful – it still was, yet now also appeared utterly exhausted and overwhelmed by sadness.

It was almost as if the misery of Palestine's tortured existence had superimposed itself on top of the memory of the sweet, gorgeous face she remembered Mariam once had.

Hanan was having trouble correlating the woman she saw before her now with the way she remembered her. "I'm haunted by you, Mariam, I keep dreaming of you," she replied. "Remembering our past... what could have been."

Hanan's eyes suddenly welled up as she grew more emotional.

At that exact moment there was a power cut and Hanan instantly vanished from Mariam's screen as her computer crashed.

Mariam looked out the window at the camp. It was still fully lit under the Israeli military's floodlights.

Her mind drifted off, to the past, as she stared into the distance, her focus entirely on *The Wall*.

3

-.-. --- -. -. . -.-. - .. -. --.

JERUSALEM, ISRAEL | SYDNEY, AUSTRALIA

O N THE OTHER side of that same twenty-nine-foot concrete wall, Esther looked out of her bedroom window in Jerusalem. She could see the botanical gardens in the distance and also the glassy surface of the lake in the gardens where she used to enjoy playing as a child.

Esther's home was in the neighborhood of Neve Granot. Although it was literally only a few miles west of Aida Refugee Camp, her apartment on Avraham Granot Street was in Israel where life was much more prosperous and free than life in Palestine's West Bank.

Esther had barely gotten out of bed even though she had woken at eight o'clock that morning. That was about two hours ago and yet it felt like two minutes.

What... just... happened?

Like many moments during this eerie quarantine period, Esther didn't know where the time had gone and could barely recall what she'd even been thinking about during those two hours. Since the nationwide Coronavirus lockdown had been ordered by Israeli Prime Minister Benjamin Netanyahu earlier in the year, she felt like her feet had never really touched the ground. There had been this hypnotic, dream-like quality to all of her days.

Isolated from her local friends, and unable to visit her elderly parents at their home in a Tel Aviv retirement village, thirty-eight-year-old Esther had been alone with her thoughts a lot lately. That was something she usually tried to avoid at all costs.

Esther had been diagnosed with depression and today was one of those days she felt that hideous black cloud hovering over her head. She knew from experience there was nothing she could do to alleviate it.

Even the antidepressants her doctor had prescribed usually just took the hit off the mental anguish slightly. Besides, she tried to avoid such pharmaceutical drugs for she feared either getting addicted to them or else experiencing their negative side effects.

To make matters worse, the Israeli also suffered from post-traumatic stress disorder, or PTSD. The trauma stemmed from being the survivor of a Palestinian terrorist attack in her teenage years.

Exactly two decades later she still had regular flashbacks to the ghastly incident which had left several in her town injured – *and* her best friend, Abigail, dead. Esther remembered the moment like it was yesterday. It had started out a joyful occasion as she had been attending an eighteenth birthday party with Abigail. A Palestinian rocket landed nearby. Abigail was among those who were struck, and a stunned Esther was left holding her friend in her arms as she died. That moment of unexpected horror had altered her personality irrevocably.

Today was the twentieth anniversary of Abigail's death and Esther planned to light a candle to commemorate her childhood friend. Even though she wasn't a practicing Jew anymore, the yahrtzeitlicht was one custom in Judaism she still adhered to.

Once dressed, Esther walked around her apartment. She turned on her radio in the kitchen and to her annoyance there was immediately a mention of Palestinian extremists. The news report mentioned how Hamas, the Palestinian Sunni-Islamic fundamentalist militant organization governing the Gaza Strip, was planning terrorist actions to coincide with upcoming Jewish holidays.

She felt irritated but not because she hated hearing about Israel's thorn in its side, Palestine. Rather, it was only because the mention of terror attacks often triggered her PTSD symptoms such as anxiety or even skin rashes.

Esther hastily changed the radio's station to try to not only get her mind off the topic, but also avoid listening to Israeli journalists who she all too often disagreed with.

Unlike many of her fellow citizens, she considered herself an unbiased, clear-headed observer of the Middle East conflict. In fact, she felt her unique, varied background gave her advantages over many other Israelis.

A legal aid to a children's defense lawyer by profession, she held a master's degree in human rights in addition to her law degree. Esther had also worked in Europe previously and had seen much of the world as a tourist, journeying as far away as Australia.

Like many Israelis, she was a descendant of Holocaust survivors. Three of her four now deceased grandparents had all endured imprisonment in Nazi concentration camps during the Second World War. She took the phrase "Never Forget" seriously and by studying the Holocaust, and listening to the accounts of her grandparents and other survivors, she believed she had gained a deep understanding of not only the relentless nature of anti-Semitism, but also how genocides were *allowed* to happen.

All this diverse life experience gave her the confidence to believe she understood much of the complexity, or multifaceted nature, of human behavior – and the plethora of reasons why armed conflicts and human rights abuses occurred.

Despite being the survivor of a Palestinian terrorist attack herself, Esther knew the extremists who caused such atrocities were only an evil anomaly and in her opinion did not remotely represent all Palestinian people. Especially as she also knew around fifty percent of all Palestinians were children.

Beyond all the usual arguments over history, territorial claims, ethnic origins and religion, the bottom line for Esther was the way Palestinians were being treated was just not kosher. In fact, it was an abomination. But what could she do? She was only one of millions of Israeli voters.

As she began to make herself a cup of coffee, Esther tried to think of something else. But in the end, she reluctantly thought further about the Israel-Palestine conflict.

To her mind, the Far Right ultra-nationalists, or hardcore Zionists as they were colloquially called in Israeli society and abroad, were among the biggest problems within her nation.

Such extreme patriots, as far as she could tell, did not believe in a two-state solution even if they sometimes said they did. After all, these same people fully supported the settlers who controversially claimed more and more Palestinian land, year after year, in the West Bank.

In elections, she usually voted for Meretz – a secular, Left-wing party comprised of both Jews and Arabs. One of Meretz's main goals was to deliver a fair two-state solution which would resemble the roughly fifty-fifty split in the Israel-Palestine borders from many decades earlier. The progressive political party was also for social justice and increased human rights, especially for ethnic minorities.

As Esther stirred her coffee, she opened a two-day-old copy of *The Jerusalem Post* newspaper. She immediately bypassed all articles related to Coronavirus as by now she had COVID-19 overload. Eventually she came across a headline that interested her a little more. It read, 'Russian Billionaire Medvedev donates $100m to Israeli settler group'.

As she sipped the steaming hot coffee, Esther skimmed the newspaper article. She noticed it quoted the Jewish Russian billionaire Medvedev who cited Biblical excerpts supporting his assertion that Israeli settlers were "justified in claiming" Palestinian sites on the West Bank.

Not being religious, Esther felt repulsed by such Jewish fundamentalists. She felt that anyone quoting "history" from the Torah in relation to the Middle East Conflict could go jump in Lake Tiberias. Using Biblical accounts – whether true, false or somewhere in between – to attempt to condone unjust treatment of Palestinians was again not kosher in her opinion.

Furthermore, she despised the recent development of what she considered an extremist, religious, uber-patriotic class. For she sensed they were slowly but surely re-orientating Israeli society into a scary theocracy.

Esther felt sure that any time Israel annexed more land or used illegal methods to expand its borders, it not only created more Palestinian victims; it also led to more Jewish victims.

God knows I am one of them, she thought. That was because she felt sure the rocket attack which had killed Abigail was in direct response to hardline Israeli military measures days earlier.

What's more, she considered such illegal, aggressive or unnecessary behavior by Israel also increased anti-Semitism worldwide. All too often, people confused the Israeli military or Far Right aspects in the government with the nature of Jewish people. To Esther's mind, that unique form of anti-Semitic hatred, where ultra-Zionism got conflated with Jewish identity, was as idiotic as hating all Americans or all Christians just because the US military had seemingly started numerous unnecessary wars since WW2.

However, she was aware for people worldwide who were not well versed in Jewish culture, Judaism or Middle East politics, it was an all too common mistake that was bound to continue.

Esther genuinely wanted a two-state solution and believed that was the *only* solution to ever achieve peace. Historical debates about how or when Palestinians had arrived in the region, or arguments about ethnic origins, were to her akin to the shouting matches between petulant, self-entitled children in inheritance disputes.

Conversely, she also felt that much of the conflict could be blamed on failures of the Palestinian leadership. And this wounded not only Israelis, but also Palestinians themselves. Esther knew that those in Israel and the West who thought like her and were actually serious about peace, and who were willing to compromise and negotiate, had been road-blocked too often by inflexible Palestinian politicians.

In fact, their terrorist tactics, although only usually carried out by extremists and not ordinary, everyday Palestinians, were not helping the Palestinian cause at all. Nor was Islamic fundamentalism which irked Esther as much as religious fanaticism in her nation.

Having finished her coffee, she put the newspaper aside and walked over to the sink. As she washed the cup, her thoughts turned to a mysterious and unexpected Facebook message she'd received two days earlier.

Around that same moment in time, Levi stared into his laptop's webcam in the lounge of his apartment in Sydney, Australia. He raised his finger to start a video call, before hesitating at the last second.

Levi felt uncertain of himself as he caught a reflection of his face in the laptop's screen.

A Jewish Aussie, he was a handsome thirty-nine-year-old who still appeared quite boyish. Being a Sephardic Jew, he had dark hair, dark brown eyes and olive skin.

He hesitated further and somehow felt he needed to psych himself up for what he was about to do. Or try to do.

Levi jumped up, grabbed a pair of dumb-bells and executed a dozen quick curls to pump his biceps. Flexing his muscles and adjusting his hair in a mirror hanging on the facing wall, he cleared his throat a few times then sat back down on his couch.

He mentally told himself to grow a pair before forcing himself to finally start the video call. He felt twitchy as the call rang and rang without any response.

Levi's heart skipped a beat as the call was suddenly answered and Esther appeared in the kitchen of her home in Jerusalem, Israel.

Before even saying a word, Esther smiled and waved into her camera. Levi waved back.

"Hi Levi, how are you?"

"Hey Esther!" Levi exclaimed. "Wow... You look barely a year older than how I remember you!"

"Yeah, right... I got old too."

There was an awkward pause between them.

"So," Esther continued then paused again for a moment. "I was very surprised to see your name in my Facebook messages the other day. What's it been, like twenty years almost?"

"Um, eighteen I think," Levi replied.

"Wow, where did our lives go?" Esther chuckled.

Levi laughed as he observed the same fantastic smile he'd always remembered her for. Her warm, green eyes and the fair skin common to Ashkenazi Jews seemed just as visually alluring to him as they had almost two decades earlier. He wasn't concerned that she'd aged, because; one, she'd aged gracefully, and; two, he'd already looked carefully at her latest selfies on her Facebook profile. And he'd figured out that she still really turned him on.

Levi also loved the short, bob hairdo she'd now adopted, not to mention that she'd gotten bustier and curvier since he'd last known her – and Lord knew Levi loved good curves on a lady.

Truth be told, as much as he had adored the girly version of Esther he once knew, he was even more attracted to the womanly version he saw on his screen staring back at him.

"I'm just reaching out to everyone to see if they're okay during this time," Levi said as a way to keep the conversation flowing. "So how're you doing?"

"I'm okay," Esther said. "Just stuck here at home and staying safe like everyone else."

Over the next five minutes, the pair engaged in similar introductory questions and answers. They began to catch up on each other's lives in the many years since last knowing each other.

Esther discovered Levi had been busy managing restaurants on behalf of entrepreneurs. He had worked around Australia and in several countries throughout Asia. To her surprise he'd never gotten married. Levi blamed his constant relocating as the reason for this.

What wasn't being discussed within their conversation was that Levi and Esther were former lovers.

They had dated for eighteen months in their late teens, having met when Levi spent a year in Israel working in the hospitality sector in hotels in Tel Aviv and Jerusalem. Following that, Esther had moved back to Australia to be with him. After a year the relationship came to an end and Esther moved back to Israel. They had never seen or even communicated with each other since.

Esther eventually became conscious of the time, especially as she was planning to properly commemorate the anniversary of Abigail's death before the day was over. She looked at Levi on her screen and politely gestured to him as if she was waiting for a punch line.

"So… um… why have you actually contacted me, Levi?"

Levi took a deep breath as he stared at her. He prepared to reveal something deeply important to him. Something he hoped Esther would resonate with.

"Well, I… " Levi's voiced cracked. He cleared his throat once more. "I guess during this lockdown... my mind drifted back to the past... and I found myself thinking of you, in detail."

4

-.-. --- -. -. . -.-. - .. -. --.

AUCKLAND, NEW ZEALAND | ZÜRICH, SWITZERLAND

THE QUEUE AT Starbucks on Queen Street was longer than Byron had expected it to be. About two dozen people were queuing outside the café on Auckland's main street on this near freezing morning.

Byron had a beanie on his head and also wore a long coat. He'd heard on the radio before leaving home that there was snow down south on the Desert Road. Every Kiwi who lived in New Zealand's North Island knew that snowfall in that region usually meant colder-than-usual temperatures combined with nasty wind chills. But still, as he felt the bitter southerly wind blast into his face, he couldn't help but curse inwardly.

Byron had arrived in downtown Auckland shortly after six o'clock that morning. He was expecting to be able to grab a quick coffee before catching a bus to the nearby inner city suburb of Ponsonby.

However, Byron had forgotten that the city was now in lockdown for the second time in 2020. Due to small clusters of new confirmed cases of COVID-19, the nation's Prime

Minister Jacinda Ardern had ordered the citywide shutdown the previous afternoon.

The underrated intricacies of lockdowns made daily life laborious to say the least. One example, which Byron was dealing with at that moment, was that everyone grabbing a takeaway coffee still had to provide their name and details, even if they only stepped into the store for a few minutes. Furthermore, instead of having every staff member focus on making coffees, one staffer, here at Starbucks at least, was tasked with ensuring everyone in the queue kept a minimum of six feet apart as part of strict social distancing measures.

All customers in the queue were also wearing masks. Byron was too, albeit reluctantly. He had endured an undiagnosable yet severe lung condition only a year or so earlier, and even though he was now healthy he worried mask wearing could possibly trigger a relapse. That concerned him as much or more than potentially catching the virus.

Once he had navigated his way through all the Coronavirus measures in place and was finally served in the café, he walked to a nearby bus stop with coffee in hand.

As he waited for a bus with several other commuters, Byron had time to think. Like many Kiwis, he was still trying to process what the hell was happening this year to his beloved New Zealand. Furthermore, he had had a rollercoaster life, mostly full of downs, in the last few years before the global pandemic had begun.

Today was his thirty-eighth birthday, but in many ways he felt like he was just starting from scratch. And that wasn't a good thing for he was operating at a bare minimum at a time in his life when he needed stability to buy a house and perhaps start a family. He had close to zero savings in the bank and somehow had to find a way to generate a consistent income.

Worse, he didn't feel he had the same energy as young adults beginning their working lives. Even though he had experience on his side, he also felt nervous competing against a younger work force. The *kids*, as he called the younger generation, all seemed more tech-savvy, more positive and less broken emotionally.

Since being fired from a high paying position as a journalist in Australia in 2018, and then losing his mother in 2019, he had been at the lowest ebb in his life to date.

He'd moved back to his native New Zealand shortly before the Coronavirus pandemic began. The timing had made it difficult to secure any jobs in print journalism, or any form of journalism for that matter. Strangely, nobody seemed to be interviewing even though the news business was booming like never before.

Byron's bus arrived on time, but for some reason the door remained closed after it parked in the bus bay. The driver eventually indicated he was not ready to allow Byron or any of the other commuters on board yet.

As he was forced to wait even longer out in the nasty southerly wind, Byron suddenly caught his own reflection in one of the windows of the bus. It was the first time in many months that he'd actually looked at himself. Tall and lean with dark hair and mysterious green eyes, he had the look of someone who didn't quite belong. There was something a bit otherworldly about him.

Byron looked away from his reflection as the driver finally opened the doors and allowed him to jump on the bus along with several other passengers.

Once he took a seat, he checked out a few files on his phone. They were files relating to the self-employment venture he was cautiously beginning on a shoestring budget.

Because of necessity rather than choice, he had recently ventured into citizen journalism as an online business. It was the best idea he could come up with during this enforced period of isolation, even if he was unsure whether it would yield any dividends. He knew he had to try something.

Byron studied the Sky Tower and its adjoining casino from his window seat as the bus slowly passed Wellesley Street West. As it continued on its way out of downtown Auckland, he couldn't help noticing the depressing gray dome of cloud cover hanging over the city. It kind of matched his mood.

After disembarking from his bus in the popular restaurant suburb of Ponsonby, Byron walked half a mile before arriving at his destination on Hukanui Crescent – the Kelmarna Organic Community Gardens. The urban community farm and associated gardens was the entire reason for his outing on this day. He loved visiting the almost five acres of vegetable plots, livestock and beehives. It was a weekly sojourn he somehow needed to experience. In fact, it had become even more important to him during this year of social distancing, lockdowns and general isolation measures.

Byron purchased a jar of organic honey at the onsite shop then grabbed a basket and sauntered off to pick some organic vegetables in one of the veggie gardens.

There was suddenly a break in the gray cloud cover overhead and the sun shone through. At that moment the southerly wind abated slightly and Byron noticed even the cows near him looked grateful for the respite.

A large blue butterfly appeared before his face. It was a brilliant shade of blue, iridescent and luminous. He knew nothing about the science of butterflies, but he found it a bit odd that one was out during New Zealand's late winter. He couldn't remember ever having seen butterflies other than during the spring and summer months.

Byron didn't know that while most species of butterflies spent winter hidden away developing during their formative period, others like the Monarch migrated thousands of miles to warmer climes, and a precious few species emerged towards the end of winter – even when snow was still on the ground.

The magnificent blue butterfly flapped its wings as it flew away.

Almost instinctively, he decided to take a break and lie down on the earth. As he listened to the sounds of nature, including children playing in a field close to him, and the chirping of birds, he remembered some unusual night-time experiences he'd had lately. They were so perplexing he'd had difficulty comprehending what exactly had transpired. However, as he looked up at the rays of morning sunlight bursting through the clouds above, he began to sense one or two truths at least about these strange after dark occurrences.

Byron had been having out of body experiences regularly since being forced to spend so much time alone during the lockdowns. These nightly "trips" were frustrating as much as they were mind-expanding as they were entirely involuntary and not something he had remotely tried to achieve. Given he was trying to solve his employment and financial situations, these ethereal experiences were also a massive distraction.

The mystical happenings had all started immediately after he watched a late night movie. It was the classic WW2 film, *The Great Escape*. The epic was screening on commercial television and with all the ad breaks it lasted almost four hours.

Byron had been so exhausted by the time he went to bed that he expected to be asleep within seconds. Instead, as soon as he had closed his eyes he found himself hovering over his body and floating within his bedroom. He was fully conscious and realized he was looking down in horror at his physical self.

On that first occasion, the out of body experience ended almost as soon as it had begun. Byron woke up like a scared, young child hearing a noise in the middle of the night. He immediately turned his bedside lamp on and jumped out of bed.

What the... Like, seriously, WHAT THE... ?!

That had been about all he could say or think as he stood there alone in his apartment. He didn't know what had just happened, nor did he have any context for it. He'd never read any literature about spiritual matters and had always considered himself an agnostic.

I'll find out when I die, was his father's motto and Byron subscribed to it to also. He believed it was a waste of time to consider whether there was an afterlife or anything beyond the Earthly realm. It made sense to him that nobody could ever know any conclusive answers until they died and either each person would awaken in some other world, or they would be extinct forever like the atheists believed.

But over the next few weeks the out of body experiences had continued. They often began the same way, with him awakening in some alternative self that felt like his body but was not his physical body. He was never dreaming or asleep, for he experienced a dual consciousness state where he could feel himself awake lying in bed, but his main awareness was in this floating self.

Even though he feared he was losing his mind, Byron applied his journalistic skills to research it thoroughly. This was what he was trained to do for any new subject he wrote about and he approached this metaphysical research in the same meticulous way.

Byron was relieved to discover he was not insane – or alone for that matter. Many millions of people had reported such out of body experiences, or OOBE's, and there were all kinds of theories about OOBE's in neuroscience as well as in metaphysics. A vast amount of studies had been done on them for decades within academia, but they remained a mystery to science.

OOBE's were often referred to, Byron noted, as astral travel by mystics. They had been experienced globally, in most cultures, for many centuries. There were even Biblical era paintings depicting the soul, or astral body, or some kind of otherworldly second body, leaving the physical body during sleep or other unconscious states.

Curiously, there were many similarities between reports of OOBE's and Near Death Experiences, or NDE's. With NDE's, where the patient was clinically dead, the individual would usually report leaving their body and floating above their lifeless physical self in hospital emergency wards or in ambulances or on accident sites.

As Byron remained stretched out on the ground in the community farm and looking up at the sky, he wondered if he really had had a glimpse of life in the Great Beyond. As much as he wanted to remain extremely logically minded, it really did feel like he existed somewhere beyond the Earth during each of those magical moments spent out of his body. He didn't know where, but the best way he could describe it was it felt like he'd gone to some another dimension. A dimension he could only describe as an infinite, quantum ocean he was able to swim in.

During these OOBE's he would sometimes astral travel beyond his bedroom, beyond his apartment and elsewhere. He would essentially fly like some kind of paranormal version of superman above Auckland City. Other times his reality would instantly morph into a completely non-Earth landscape. All these experiences were while he was awake and conscious, not unconscious or asleep.

As if all that didn't sound crazy enough, something else odd had occurred. Twice he had seen a number that appeared in a shimmering blue light before his astral eyes.

987

He had no idea what the number 987 related to. He knew it was thirteen less than one thousand and wondered if that number had any significance.

Like anyone born in the Western or Christian world he knew the number thirteen was associated with being unlucky. However, after Googling numerology he discovered that it was actually a lucky number within other cultures or religions, including Judaism.

Still lying down at the urban farm, he was jolted out of his contemplative state as a small boy ran up to him. The boy's tiny foot touched Byron's face. The infant's mother quickly ran over and grabbed her son. She apologized profusely for the intrusion.

Byron took that as his cue to leave for the day. Besides, he had work to do in his new business venture.

He headed back to Queen Street, before catching a ferry across Waitematā Harbour to his home on Auckland's North Shore.

Later that day, Byron sat at his office desk in his one bedroom apartment in the harbourside suburb of Devonport.

He could just glimpse the top of a frigate of the Royal New Zealand Navy in the nearby naval base. The ensign, or national flag, could be seen fluttering in the breeze on top of the ship.

Byron had been living in Devonport for about a year since he'd split with his long-time girlfriend. He thought of her for a few seconds, wondering why that relationship had come to an end. He still didn't know. It had just kind of petered out with neither formally calling an end to the relationship.

The Kiwi journalist refocused himself on the present. He quickly read some pages with handwritten notes on them. In fact, he obsessively scanned these short-hand notes on his desk as if to mentally prepare himself.

He then clicked his mouse a few times to begin a video call.

Dignified-looking African gent, Albert, appeared on screen on the other end of the video conference. He was seated in a leather chair, in his luxurious-looking office in Zürich, Switzerland. Mahogany bookshelves were visible in the background.

Albert was in his fifties but looked both younger and older. He had youthful black skin yet his eyes looked like those of a tired, old man.

Byron greeted Albert. The two shared some formal introductions, then began to briefly discuss the podcast ahead.

Podcasting was Byron's best idea to start again since losing a high paying job as a leading journalist at the *Sydney Morning Herald* newspaper. He still had the skills to get to the bottom of complex news stories and he wanted to see if there might still be a place for him in the news world. Even if it was just in a small capacity within independent media.

Wanting to focus on important, yet underreported issues of the era, Byron had called his podcast show *Underground Knowledge*. So far he had only been able to attract a few low-level names as guests, however. They included a first-time author who had written a book about disgraced Hollywood producer Harvey Weinstein, as well as a nurse who was trying to expose medical corruption she claimed to have witnessed when the Coronavirus pandemic first began.

Unfortunately, the nurse, who was French, had a poor grasp of English; as well as being hard to understand, the first-time author seemed to favor rumors over facts.

Nobody had set the show alight, and the stories were getting lost in the untold amount of videos uploaded daily on YouTube and various social media platforms. Byron had not had many views for any of the podcast episodes, and the number of subscribers currently languished at around one thousand.

An American child rights advocate who had researched the recent capture and arrest of Ghislaine Maxwell – the British socialite accused of helping Jeffrey Epstein lure underage sex trafficking victims – had then agreed to appear on the show before cancelling at the last hour.

Byron had been considering giving up on podcasting, when out of the blue a British banker had contacted him to say

Albert had wanted to appear on the show. Byron was surprised given Albert was a well-known financial commentator and a *New York Times* bestselling author who could've appeared on any news media in the world. Regardless, it was quite a lucky break and he knew he had to seize the opportunity.

In their pre-interview discussion, Byron told Albert some basic things like the length of the podcast interview, types of questions that he planned to ask and the discussion style.

Byron talked to Albert with utmost respect and thanked him for offering to be a guest on the podcast. Albert was very gentlemanly and accommodating, not arrogant. They immediately seemed to strike up a good rapport.

Once all that was out of the way, Byron went to hit the record button to begin the podcast. Just before he could however, Albert signaled to Byron which caused him to pause.

"I just have one request please," Albert said. He had a strong African accent. Byron was aware it was Ghanaian in fact.

"Sure, anything you wish."

"At the start, immediately after we go live before your audience... I'd like to reveal something... Just a little surprise."

Byron was a little bemused, but nodded his approval anyway.

"I could tell you what it's about now, of course," Albert added. "However, I believe it is more in alignment with my new life path for the world to see us work through the past together... Live and unfiltered... in the moment."

Byron continued to nod to Albert, but internally he was trying to read between the lines.

"A cautionary word to the wise," Albert said, "if you will."

5

-.-. --- -. -. . -.-. - .. -. --.

WUHAN, CHINA | HOUSTON, USA

FRESH FACED, PLATINUM-blonde haired, nineteen-year-old Emma hastily shared a new conspiracy video report she'd just come across on alternative media. Her fingers were a blur as she crisscrossed various social media and messaging accounts using a variety of apps on her phone.

She added her own summary for the video on each platform, all typed in short-hand text understood by the Generation Z crowd.

This included ROFL for *Rolling on floor laughing*, SMH for *Shaking my head*, IKR for *I know, right*, and ?4U for *I have a question for you*. She also inserted various emoji faces, memes and GIFs to visually convey certain points.

Within a few minutes Emma had successfully shared the video with thousands of online friends across social media sites such as Snapchat, Twitter, Facebook and Instagram, as well as encrypted messaging services like WhatsApp, Viber, Telegram and Signal. She also spread it on Chinese platforms she'd recently signed up to, including WeChat and Sina Weibo.

Being born in San Francisco in 2001 and growing up in the internet age, Emma felt in her element constantly operating in this maelstrom of technology. Like most other Gen Z-ers, engaging virtually with people online via phones and other devices felt totally natural.

The self-assured young American was weeks into Wuhan's lockdown in China's Hubei province. As she took a break in her aparthotel and fixed herself a crab and avocado sandwich, Emma shook her head and even laughed at her current situation. It was somehow both tragic and funny to her at the same time.

Emma had flown to Wuhan from Bangkok literally days before the central government of China had imposed an unexpected lockdown on the city and the rest of Hubei.

Unexpected, as even the World Health Organization, or WHO, had called the Chinese government's decision "unprecedented in public health history".

Having studied the Mandarin language since she was seven years old and having always been fascinated by Chinese culture, this had been Emma's long planned adventure in China before she returned to America to begin college. She had friends in Beijing, including a Chinese-American she had gone to high school with, and was originally heading there after what was supposed to have been a brief stop-over in Wuhan.

She never made it to Beijing because of the abrupt lockdown and the initial two-day stopover was now many weeks and counting.

Emma had been stuck in the room of her aparthotel in Wuhan this whole time. She was living all alone, but more connected online than ever before. As a result of setting up a virtual private network, or VPN, she had found a way to bypass the Great Firewall of China that tried to control the internet within the communist country.

Thanks to that VPN she could do anything she wanted online anonymously by "spoofing" her location – a common tactic that not only tourists visiting the nation often used, but also tech savvy Chinese citizens used as well.

Besides keeping in touch with her mother, Emma had decided to use the enforced alone time to take a deep dive down various rabbit holes. She had always been an alternative thinker who rarely believed in anything the mainstream media promoted. Now, with the strange events of 2020, it just felt like the perfect time for her to attempt to understand the way the world really worked.

Apart from evaluating written articles and watching a lot of videos online, she was also reading various non-fiction ebooks.

One title she had recently read was Sean Stone's book *New World Order: A Strategy of Imperialism* which gave her some historical perspective regarding the way imperialist power operated internationally. Before that she had read *Pharmageddon* by David Healy which put forward the idea of pharmaceuticalization of medicine.

Next, she planned to read *No Such Thing as a Free Gift: The Gates Foundation and the Price of Philanthropy* by Linsey McGoey. She had noted the book's synopsis promised to put the "new golden age of philanthropy under the microscope" and expose what it termed the massive new business sector of "philanthro-capitalism" that the likes of the Gates and Clinton foundations were apparently benefitting from.

Apart from these non-fiction titles, she was also reading classic dystopian fiction that she thought might shed some light on the state of the world. First she'd read *1984* by George Orwell then *Brave New World* by Aldous Huxley. She was currently reading *We* by Yevgeny Zamyatin – a little known novel published in 1921 that was said to have directly influenced both *1984* and *Brave New World*.

One of her favorite quotes so far in *We* was about the balance of free will of individuals versus what was best for society. "The only means of ridding man of crime is ridding him of freedom." Emma instinctively felt that quote from the novel was philosophically true. She believed at a certain point technology, with the likes of drones and other surveillance tech as well as AI, would evolve to such an extent where eradicating all or at least most crime would become possible.

In Emma's opinion, there would be a massive catch to this crime prevention technology. She felt sure that the supposedly utopian society of the future would come at the cost of restricting the freedoms of individuals.

Another quote in the novel implied to Emma much the same thing: "Those two, in paradise, were given a choice: happiness without freedom, or freedom without happiness. There was no third alternative..."

There was one additional statement in Zamyatin's novel that spoke to her even more than all the other profound quotes within the story. In fact, it was as if the almost century-old book was reading her mind: "The knife is the most durable, immortal, the most genius thing that man created. The knife was the guillotine; the knife is the universal means of solving all knots; and along the blade of a knife lies the path of paradox – the single most worthy path of the fearless mind."

Ah, paradox! That thing that everyone is afraid of!

Emma believed she had seen evidence of this online where most of the Sheeple, as she called mainstream thinkers, were petrified of paradoxical concepts. They wanted arguments to be neatly summarized in black and white terms. They attacked anyone who tried to infuse contradictory concepts into online debates, even if the person was on their side overall.

But just as she resonated with what this old Russian novel was conveying to her, Emma wanted to walk the path of paradox and become the "fearless mind" Zamyatin referred to. Paradoxical thoughts were what furthered her mind for they contained shades of all arguments. And this was why Emma freely posted her thoughts online without regard to what label or term people saddled her with. She didn't care about the Left-Right political paradigm or economic categories like capitalism or socialism or any other isms.

Some strangers online, and even some of her friends, regularly called her a conspiracy theorist, but she didn't care about being labeled that either. After all, Emma didn't give a flying fuck what Sheeple thought. In fact, she viewed many of their insults as evidence she was on exactly the right path.

They've yet to learn the only difference between conspiracy theory and conspiracy fact, she reminded herself, *is six months.*

Emma also felt sure that 2020 was more like conspiracy reality than mere theory, where everything nefarious and hidden was slowly becoming obvious. So much so that she had taken to calling the year the *Great Sheeple Awakening* where every Normie (her alternative term for Sheeple) was being forced to "wake the fuck up" as she wrote in one Facebook post.

Even though she was researching various topics, COVID-19 had become her pet subject. Especially as she had now observed the virus spread beyond China's borders and affect much of the rest of the world, including her home state of Texas.

Having now finished making her crab and avocado sandwich, Emma sat back down on a sofa by a window. She scanned her recent posts and was surprised to see just how many related to the virus.

Headings included: *Are the lockdowns and quarantines about something more than just the virus?*; *Is Coronavirus (COVID-19) a man-made lab creation?*; *The privacy, censorship, legal, financial and human rights ramifications of Coronavirus*; *The COVID World Order begins*; *Is the 2020 Corona saga a psy-op designed to modify human behavior?*; *Doctors and Medical Scientists with contrarian opinions on the new Coronavirus; Can Tedros Adhanom (the WHO head honcho) be trusted?; What's the worst case scenario of the over(CORONA)reaction?.*

Many of her other posts, likes and shares were associated with Coronavirus conspiracy subjects. These included planned 5G theories, predictions about mandatory vaccinations, as well as depopulation agenda she personally believed Bill Gates subscribed to.

Emma was also a follower of the highly controversial QAnon – an ever-evolving conspiracy theory that claimed a globalist cabal was plotting against President Donald Trump.

She had as a result recently changed her mind on Trump. Previously, she'd always seen him as a narcissistic asshole and she still basically did.

However, upon reading further and diving deeper down her research rabbit holes, she had come to believe Trump even with all his faults was a positive tool of sorts. A tool that was being used to restore many constitutional rights that had been lost to Americans in the post WW2 era.

She also believed Trump was on a secret mission to end child-trafficking exactly as QAnon stated. To Emma, he was a demolition-man slowly destroying the Deep State or the criminal, elitist elements within the US Government.

Having now finished her sandwich, Emma took a rare look away from her phone. She stared out her window at the deserted streets of the usually bustling, city of Wuhan. Even though she knew it had a population of eleven million people, Wuhan looked like a ghost town.

Later that day, half a world away in Houston, Texas, Emma's mother Heather was trying to keep up with the myriad of conspiracy theories coming her way. Phone in hand, the thirty-seven-year-old stood on her apartment balcony as she listened to her daughter rabbiting on and on.

Emma could see downtown Houston's streets below, as well as the city skyline, that were all visible in the background behind her mother. It made her feel more homesick than ever.

"Just need to hang in there, Em," Heather said.

On the political level it was not a case of like mother, like daughter, as, unlike Emma, Heather despised Trump and prayed he would be replaced in the November election. She felt certain Trump was a natural agent of chaos who was destroying the foundations of the USA with what she viewed as a complete disrespect for ordinary, everyday, hard-working Americans.

"Yes, don't worry Mom," Emma replied. "I'm still fine... I'm just, like, shocked that I'm in this position."

Heather nodded her understanding. She knew her daughter was exhibiting strength outwardly, but deep down she also knew Emma just wanted to be back home and safe in her arms again.

Given Chinese authorities had told her daughter she probably wouldn't be able to return to America for several more weeks if not months, Heather knew Emma was also scared. Yet she didn't want to mention this or express more fear on top of all the worries Emma already had.

Instead, Heather took a more nuanced approach. She showed great compassion for her daughter as a typically empathetic mother, yet stayed very calm. She also tried to get Emma to focus on possible solutions and remain hopeful, rather than fixating on the very obvious problems.

Emma eventually shifted her concern to her mother. Her mom lived alone and she worried about her too.

"What about you Mom, are you alright there?"

"Yes. Don't worry about me at all. I am just staying indoors mostly since this virus reached here too."

6

-.-. --- -. -. . -.-. - .. -. --.

LONDON, UK | BALI, INDONESIA

MARK TOOK A final drag of his cigarette before throwing it to the ground and beginning his walk home.

The tall, blue eyed, slightly graying, forty-one-year-old Englishman was dressed in a suit and tie. He had just had a business meeting on nearby Kensington High Street and had decided to then have an afternoon stroll through London's Hyde Park.

As he exited the park via Kensington Gardens, Mark lit up another cigarette. He reluctantly forced himself to think about some of the issues he needed to sort out in his life.

Unlike many of his fellow Brits, navigating the ongoing Coronavirus saga was not the biggest challenge he was facing. Instead, his dilemmas were mostly within his South Kensington home.

He had a marriage that was possibly falling apart or possibly about to be mended. Mark didn't even know anymore what stage his relationship with his wife was at. He and Vicky had been in marriage counselling for several weeks before Britain's nationwide COVID-19 lockdown had halted proceedings.

To complicate matters even further, Vicky had recently found out she was pregnant. Yet, she'd also revealed that given the uncertain and somewhat volatile state of their marriage, she didn't know whether she wanted to give birth. Abortion, she'd said, had not been ruled out.

Additionally his normally successful events management business required attention. He had already had to let two part-time staff go and it was impossible to plan anything for the future. Most events had been cancelled or else postponed for months.

The government was providing the company a financial relief package to keep it afloat, but Mark hated relying on the government for anything. Especially as he prided himself on being the type of guy who always made things happen.

Worst of all, his sister had died in a car accident three days into the lockdown. That tragedy had left him with an additional dilemma: what to do with the six-year-old niece he had temporarily adopted.

To give himself some hope, he had told himself the adoption was only temporary. However, given how unreliable his only brother was, he knew the adoption would probably end up permanent. His long-lost brother was abroad playing at being a hippy and Mark assumed he just didn't have fatherhood in him.

Not that he disliked his niece, Sophie, at all. She was a sweet child who had just lost her mother and had no known father. It was simply that Mark, and his wife-for-now Vicky, were not in the right mental state to adopt a child. In fact, they had already been in a daze before Sophie had come into their lives.

As Mark headed along Gloucester Road in the direction of the River Thames, he was surprised to see a group of protesters coming toward him.

When the group neared he saw it was a Black Lives Matter, or BLM, protest. The protestors were chanting "black lives matter" over and over and sounded angry.

Mark noticed they also held signs of a face he vaguely recognized from TV news broadcasts. It was the face of George Floyd, the recently deceased African-American killed in a ghastly manner by US police during an arrest.

He had not been devoting much time to following the news lately, especially stories occurring across the pond in America. So he had only paid scant attention to the murder of Floyd.

However, Mark had seen and heard enough at a glance to know Floyd's gruesome death was a major news story causing ripples the world over. He was also aware some of these racial equality protestors in Britain and America had begun pulling down statues of historical figures who in some cases had also been supporters of slavery.

He stood aside as the BLM marchers occupied the entire footpath, and was forced to wait several minutes before they all finally passed.

Walking further along Gloucester Road he eventually reached his apartment building on Cranley Gardens in South Kensington. The building was just near the corner of the fairly busy Old Brompton Road, yet somehow it had a quiet serenity to it – a result perhaps of the large trees hanging over it.

Mark hesitated for a moment. He could feel a headache coming on and wondered if he might need to soon take an aspirin.

He sighed as he looked up through the trees at the balcony of his fourth floor apartment.

Late that evening, after his wife had put their niece to bed and then retired for the evening herself, Mark began an overdue video call from his office study.

He was in the middle of what was fast becoming a fairly heated chat with his brother, Elijah, in Bali, Indonesia.

Mark felt nothing but contempt as he looked at his baby brother on his monitor.

Only six years younger than me, yet you still haven't become a real man, you useless twat.

Mark caught a glimpse of his own reflection in a mirror of his office then looked back at his brother who was hanging out on a beach somewhere in Bali. He couldn't help but notice the two of them looked like chalk and cheese. Elijah seemed almost wild and bohemian, while Mark appeared to be a model citizen-type right down to his short back and sides haircut.

"But this is a trend with you Elijah, not just one event... You weren't there for so many key family moments... Not even for our sister's funeral!"

Elijah had only minutes earlier apologized for not returning for their sister's funeral, pointing out that there were no flights currently leaving Indonesia. However, Mark wasn't really listening. He had been lied to too many times by Elijah. On top of that, Elijah to him was just one annoyance too many and he had zero patience for his brother's excuses and nonchalance.

"And on those very few times you actually were around," Mark continued, "you still weren't really there... In your head, you were always just... gone."

Elijah closed his eyes and breathed deeply.

Mark observed his brother who looked like he was entering some kind of trance-like meditation. He snapped his fingers then pointed accusingly at Elijah on the monitor.

"You see, you're even doing it now... This is exactly the same as before. You're tuning out. You're emotionally constipated. You won't engage in family issues that need resolving."

Elijah suddenly opened his eyes again.

Calm, he looked at his older brother with an apparent clarity in his eyes that Mark couldn't help but notice.

PART TWO

FACE2FACE

"Spend too long looking in
Looking in from the outside
Now it's time to give in
Time to get inside"

–Adrian Borland
| The Sound, *Hothouse*

7

.._-. ._- -._-. . .._--- .._-. ._- -._-. .

SYDNEY, AUSTRALIA | JERUSALEM, ISRAEL

IT WAS A bright, blue-sky day in Sydney. Levi was walking outside not far from his local neighborhood of Coogee in Sydney's Eastern Suburbs. He had a day off from the restaurant he worked at and wanted to get some sun on his skin as well as some exercise.

Levi was in the middle of another video chat on his smartphone with Esther. Because of the time difference, it was well after midnight in Israel. Esther was lying on her couch in the lounge of her Jerusalem apartment. She had a blanket wrapped around her and held a cup of soup from which Levi could see hot steam rising.

"So how are you holding up in this quarantine, Esther?" Levi asked. He was slightly out of breath as he walked and talked. He held his phone at waist level and looked down into its camera lens. "Have you got any friends or family nearby at least? Or are you living there all alone?"

Esther felt slightly suspicious of Levi's line of questioning. It didn't help that his phone's camera was shaking slightly as he walked. He was also often looking away, presumably at traffic, which made it hard to read his facial expressions.

This was the second video call Esther had accepted from Levi. The first one, just the previous morning, had been cut short at her insistence due to needing to commemorate the death of her childhood friend, Abigail.

Carrying out the Yarshzevlit to remember Abigail – as well as lighting candles in the memory of others she knew had been killed by Palestinian terrorists on that same day twenty years earlier – meant she still hadn't gotten to the bottom of why Levi had suddenly contacted her again.

"I live alone," she said. "And no family here in Jerusalem, just a few friends here in my neighborhood."

"Really? Are you doing okay then?"

"I'm fine," Esther replied.

That wasn't true as her depression had been intense in the last day or so and she'd barely been able to move or think clearly.

Esther began to scratch an intense itch on her cheek as she stared at her laptop where Levi's ever-smiling face and eyes stared back at her.

She could feel a rash coming on, which was one of the most common stress symptoms she experienced with her PTSD. Commemorating Abigail's death had brought back too many flashbacks of that horrific rocket attack she had survived as a teenager.

As Levi reached Coogee Beach and sat down at a seat on the grass overlooking the sea, they discussed further how the COVID-19 lockdown had been so far for each of them. Talking not only about how weird and unexpected it all was, but also about the plethora of feelings they had experienced. Both mentioned fear, loneliness, boredom and confusion, juxtaposed with unexpected clarity at times and even epiphanies.

Esther also decided to reveal to Levi that she now suffered from depression and PTSD, which was making the lockdown all the more difficult. She mentioned she was having trouble sleeping and often found herself lying awake at night feeling the uncertainty of her own future.

"The state of the world," she added, "and the constant bombardment of negative news, is somehow all manifesting on a personal level in my mind."

Levi nodded, indicating he could relate.

Esther studied Levi perceptively for a moment. He looked at her curiously and smiled once more.

"So where are you actually at, Levi?" she asked. "Emotionally... Or psychologically, I guess I mean?"

"Well, with this forced isolation period... For the first time since I was young, I've actually had time to think... and breathe... As my mind has been still instead of being consumed by work, paying bills, even relationships... So I've taken timeout from the world, really."

"Yeah, I know what you mean," Esther replied. Even though she was battling her past traumas, there was paradoxically also a part of her that was feeling calmer than she had felt in a while. She felt this was mainly because of not having to work at her law firm for the time being as the Israeli government was essentially paying her to stay at home.

"In many ways," Levi continued, "this lockdown has been the most liberating experience I've ever had. I'm sleeping better and more naturally than I have in so many years... And freed from the Monday-to-Friday nine-to-five ritual has meant I've lost track of the days... So much so that not only do I not know what day it is anymore, but I also don't care! I'm getting more exercise, drinking less, losing weight, eating better, and spending more time on things that are important or interesting to me. I feel more sense of purpose, or at least I'm clearer in my mind, now that I've been ejected out of the rat race."

Esther suddenly felt a little envious of Levi's state of mind and wished she felt that good.

"And about two weeks into this whole lockdown," Levi continued, "I looked into the mirror. I took a moment to really look at my own reflection properly... Like I haven't done since I was a child."

He looked up at the sky contemplatively for a moment.

"Mirrors are freaky in a way. There's no hiding from them. And sometimes I think we are most afraid of seeing ourselves for who we really are, warts and all."

Esther was unsure where he was going with this mirror analogy. He was starting to ramble almost like he was spontaneously expressing thoughts aloud with no filter.

"Anyway," Levi said, "d'ya know what I saw staring back at me in the mirror, Esther?"

"What?"

"A phony, a schmuck... an asshole."

Esther suddenly found herself growing more fascinated by Levi as she continued to stare at him on her monitor. Even though he still seemed to be rambling, she could also sense he was trying to be genuine and honest about himself.

Levi continued, "A fake man. A boy who has never grown up, never accepted many responsibilities in life... Actually, correction... I've never accepted any responsibility for anything in my life. It was always someone else's fault, never mine, I always looked to shift the focus or blame for mistakes away from me, do you know what I mean?"

The Australian felt embarrassed admitting all this to anyone else, especially Esther. But given he'd never been honest with women in the past, and relationships had never worked out, he felt there was no harm in trying a different tact.

You're on a roll, so why stop telling the truth to her now?

Levi looked up at waves breaking on Coogee Beach as he pondered where he was at in his life. "And then suddenly,"

Levi added, "amongst all that self-loathing, I just thought of you... "

"You thought of me? What does that even mean?"

There was a tone of mild sarcasm in Esther's voice and it was not lost on Levi. He was surprised as this was not how he remembered her at all.

Then again, it's been eighteen years and I don't even know this woman anymore!

He wondered if, perhaps, her tone might be evidence of walls she'd built up in her persona as some kind of defense mechanism.

"What I mean is," Esther added. "That doesn't add up... Why on Earth would you think of me again, now?"

8

..-. .- -.-. . ..--- ..-. .- -.-. .

RIO DE JANEIRO, BRAZIL | WEST BANK, PALESTINE

MARIAM AND HANAN were in the middle of another video chat. It had been a week since Rio-based architect Hanan had first reached out to Mariam after thirteen years of no contact between them.

Her heart went out to Mariam and all the other Palestinians who had not been able to know peace like she had. She especially felt for her fellow Christian Palestinians for they were in the minority within the Palestinian communities inside the West Bank. She knew that sometimes religious differences within Palestinians themselves caused issues or friction.

Hanan was more of a practicing Christian than Mariam. She felt that her faith had perhaps remained intact because she had gotten out of the West Bank. Fortunately for her, she had experienced a prosperous and relatively peaceful life in Brazil.

Whenever Hanan thought of Palestinians on the West Bank or in Gaza, especially ones who were living like caged dogs in refugee camps as Mariam was, she sometimes felt so traumatized and helpless she actually wanted to harm herself. A part of her always felt guilty that she had left her native land

and escaped the misery when millions of others like Mariam could not. Every joy she experienced was also tinged with an underlying sadness, for she was experiencing pleasures most of her own kind could never experience.

Like Mariam, Hanan also could not believe that the world still allowed people to live in such atrocious conditions as those in her former Palestinian communities still lived.

In particular, Hanan wanted the unlawful killings, torture and other war crimes to stop. She also wanted an end to the Israeli settlements in the West Bank which had been deemed illegal under international law for decades, yet had continued unabated all her life.

Looking at the Palestinians' miseries objectively from a world away in South America, Hanan believed there were three parties to blame for the situation. One was obviously Israel, but another was Palestinians themselves who had resorted to terrorist behavior too many times and were often inflexible or unrealistically uncompromising during peace talks. But the third party Hanan held responsible, and perhaps the most responsible of all, was the international community and the likes of the United Nations. She believed they were not forceful enough in demanding peace and resolution, nor did she sense they genuinely wanted justice for displaced Palestinians.

A quote from the Bible came to her mind regarding how the rest of the world *allowed* the Palestinians' suffering to continue: "Inasmuch as ye have done it unto one of the least of these My brethren, ye have done it unto me."

We Palestinians are the least of the Lord's people, Hanan thought. *Anything you bastards do to us, you do to God! Anytime you disrespect us, you disrespect God!*

As she conversed with Mariam, she desperately wanted to provide compensation for a past wrong she had done to her friend. A wrong that she had never forgiven herself for committing and that gnawed away at her every day. She also wanted to help a Palestinian refugee who had been victimized, tortured and abused to an almost catatonic emotional state.

"I don't want to talk about the past," Mariam snapped. "It's done, it doesn't matter now."

Her voice was hoarse and there was no warmth whatsoever in it. She spat her words out in harsh sounding Arabic.

"But it does matter, Mariam. I have more–"

"No, it doesn't!" Mariam interjected. "I have my son to look after... and my parents are very ill! Plus I've lost my English teaching job here due to this crazy Armageddon virus! So now you get in touch, expecting me to waste my time with long forgotten, irrelevant events!"

What Hanan didn't know was in the week since first contact, Mariam had had a lot more things go wrong than she was letting on.

On the same day she had become unemployed, Mariam had received news that her parents had been diagnosed with additional health conditions and faced mounting medical bills. Furthermore, things had taken yet another turn for the worse in Aida Refugee Camp.

Reports had surfaced that a hardcore Palestinian terrorist was residing in the camp, but nobody could find out who it was. As a result, Israeli soldiers had begun treating everyone like a suspect and even a disabled neighbor of Mariam's had been interrogated at length.

Additional water rations had also been imposed on the camp and none of the refugees had been given an explanation as to why.

As she thought about her ever-worsening predicament, Mariam looked out the window at the camp, or ghetto as she called it.

In front of her tiny, old, rubble-like apartment, one large military guard tower cast a giant shadow over the camp. It was built into the colossal concrete wall separating Palestine from Israel and had an ominous, all-seeing, God-like quality to it.

Overlooking the camp, the tower reminded her of a panopticon – an ingenious design concept often found in jails where a strategically-placed central guard tower was sited within a circle of prison cells. From it, guards could observe every prison inmate in every cell.

Mariam knew from reading books that the twist was the prisoners could never see the guards inside the guard tower because of the geometry of the panopticon's clever design. Consequently, the prisoners would never know whether or not they were being watched at any given moment.

Aida Refugee Camp was not designed exactly like a panopticon, but the end result was essentially the same. The refugees were always being watched, twenty four seven. Yet they could never see inside the guard tower because of its dark, tinted windows.

And the lights!

Mariam hated the lights. Floodlights in the military base on the Israeli side of the wall were so bright they were almost blinding, and they lit up every refugee home every night, all night long. It was a permanent reminder of the presence of soldiers who ruled the camp with an iron fist.

I wish I could destroy those lights! I would happily live in darkness forever!

Despite Mariam's obvious emotional fragility, Hanan persisted and managed to engage her in conversation for a few more minutes.

Hanan finally gave the apology to Mariam that she had wanted to give her for thirteen years. For it was thirteen years ago almost to the day that Hanan had come between Mariam and a local Palestinian man she'd been engaged to called Michael.

That was the day when Hanan had committed the biggest sin of her life.

At the time, Hanan had been best friends with Mariam and they even felt like sisters. Although she was not a refugee like Mariam, Hanan had worked for twelve months at Aida as part of a construction project for her architecture degree.

During that time Hanan had also begun to volunteer for various humanitarian projects within the camp. After a while, she felt her soul had become a refugee even though she was not officially classed as one. Somehow the refugees' struggle, which was even greater than that of non-refugee Palestinians, became her own struggle. She empathized with refugees that much after seeing the way Mariam and others were treated.

To her great shame however, and the awkward truth that she was now facing up to, was Hanan had deceived her best friend in the most despicable and un-Christian way.

While Mariam was pregnant with Michael's child, Hanan had an affair with Michael.

And it wasn't just sexual either. Michael claimed he'd fallen in love with Hanan and broke off his engagement with Mariam. Hanan and Michael had then left the camp and together they fled Palestine and migrated to Brazil.

At the time, Hanan had convinced herself that she and Michael were destined to marry and that Mariam was just an unfortunate casualty. That story wore thin after a while and Michael soon left Hanan after becoming enamored with a Brazilian woman.

After suffering the same fate that had befallen Mariam, Hanan came to understand just how deeply she had betrayed a good friend who had trusted her. "I am so sorry for what I did to you, Mariam."

As she stared at her fellow Palestinian on her laptop screen within her home office in Rio de Janeiro, Hanan burst into tears. Having finally apologized, it was overwhelming for her to look into the eyes of the woman she had wronged.

Mariam was anything but emotional at that moment, however. She coldly assessed Hanan's face on her own computer screen.

"You've got an inner ugliness," Mariam said. "And all your exterior beauty cannot conceal it."

Hanan was shocked by the words and felt crushed inside.

"We don't need to talk any further."

"But we do," Hanan said quickly. "I have something else I need to–"

"I have to be up early tomorrow to try to find a new job. So goodnight... and goodbye."

The screen went black at Hanan's end as Mariam abruptly terminated the video call.

Hanan continued to stare at the screen thoughtfully. She'd intended to say a lot more to Mariam, but it wasn't to be.

9

.._.-. .- -.-. . ..--- ..-. .- -.-. .

AUCKLAND, NEW ZEALAND | ZÜRICH, SWITZERLAND

SEATED IN HIS apartment's office in Auckland's naval suburb of Devonport, Byron stared at Albert's face on his monitor. The pair were on the same video call and preparing to actually begin the scheduled podcast.

Drinking coffee in the office of his Zürich home, Albert was impatient to start. He had a lot to say and wanted to get it over with.

Byron nodded to the renowned financial commentator and bestselling author as he pressed a button.

"And, we are live, I think... "

Byron scanned some opened windows on his computer screen to confirm.

"Yes, we are now streaming on YouTube, Insta, TikTok and Facebook... Welcome to another episode of Underground Knowledge! I'm your host Byron Alexander in Auckland, New Zealand, and today we have a very special guest... Albert Mensah, in Zürich, Switzerland."

Albert put his coffee aside and looked alert.

"Albert needs no introduction... But for those who've been living under a rock, Albert's the author of the bestselling book, *The New Rebels*, a book about microfinancing methods for working class people... And he singlehandedly exposed much of the corruption of the EU... Plus, he predicted Brexit, not to mention much about the virus lockdown situation we currently find ourselves in."

Albert found it funny to hear the short bio of himself. He knew he'd done all those things, yet the secret world of power he'd once been part of was something he figured many of Byron's viewers would never be able to comprehend.

Life is always different looking in as opposed to being on the inside.

However, he wanted to at least try to shed some light about the truth of the mysterious world he had spent years operating within.

"Now Albert, I have a bunch of questions to ask you... and some of our audience will also probably add some questions of their own in the live chat box... But first, I believe you have some sort of exclusive news to reveal to Undergrounders upfront?"

Albert nodded then thanked Byron for having him on the show. He also acknowledged everyone watching the live stream.

His tone abruptly changed as he transitioned into a serious subject: How Byron got fired from his print journalism position at *the Sydney Morning Herald* in 2018.

Byron was gobsmacked. He wasn't expecting to be forced to recall events of his recent past, all of which were very painful to him. He also felt very suspicious of the Ghanaian all of a sudden.

How on Earth do you know about my past and who the hell are you exactly?

Albert held up a piece of paper. Byron could see it was some kind of print-out. The older man then picked up his reading glasses.

"I have a copy here of your article, written at the Sydney Morning Herald... It's the article that got you fired... The one the paper refused to publish... It's headlined... The Invisible World Economy."

Byron still felt unsure what to say. He couldn't get a read on Albert's intentions or where all this was leading to.

Albert began to read from the body of the article. "We constantly get told there are limited resources, limited money, limited budgets available for the public's wellbeing. Yet, the truth is, the financial elites are creating the illusion of scarcity."

Albert put down the article, took off his reading glasses and looked at Byron for a full five seconds.

"You were revealing something very high level there... You were referencing Old World money… Not the one percent, but rather the top one percent of the one percent... And you were revealing that our monetary system is a gigantic Ponzi scheme! What you were here, Byron, was an uncompromising journalist trying to force a new fairer world... on behalf of the common people."

Still dumbfounded, Byron continued to stare at Albert.

"And you got chewed up and spat out," Albert continued. "Just as happens to everyone else who challenges the Establishment's narrative about the financial system."

The older man smiled, but Byron remained concerned as to where this live podcast was going. Nor did he know how to react in front of a live audience. And being new to podcasting, and broadcast journalism for that matter, didn't help.

10

..-. .- -.-. . ..--- ..-. .- -.-. .

HOUSTON, USA | WUHAN, CHINA

"YOU NEED TO try to stay calm, Emma."

It had been two days since Texan mother Heather had spoken to her Wuhan-based daughter Emma.

They had been talking daily or sometimes multiple times a day since Emma had been quarantined many weeks earlier in China's Hubei province. Heather didn't even know how many weeks ago that was as she'd lost track of time lately.

Mother and daughter had actually scheduled to have a video call three times over the last two days. Each time Heather had had to reschedule, telling Emma "something had come up".

That wasn't quite true, however. Well, something had certainly come up, but the delays were not a result of the trivial things Heather had implied they were.

Now that she was finally talking to her child, Heather was just waiting for the right moment to deliver the news.

As she listened to her fast-talking, headstrong daughter, she noticed Donald Trump on the news on her television. The TV set was on mute in the far corner of her downtown Houston apartment.

She only glimpsed Trump out of the corner of her eye, but it was a reminder that she and her daughter did not see eye to eye on their President at all.

Heather had studied personality types and psychological disorders in college and it had remained a personal interest of hers ever since. In psychoanalyzing Trump, she felt certain he was a sociopath and a narcissist.

On the political level, she was in no doubt Trump was a tyrannical authoritarian. She believed he'd made veiled threats of late and worried he would not accept the November election result were he to lose.

Heather returned her attention to her laptop monitor where Emma was talking non-stop about more conspiracy theories, including pro-Trump ones, as well as all her problems.

"I've lost my passport now, Mom!"

"What? How did you lose it?"

"In the chaos... And trust me, it is utter chaos here!"

Emma took her first break from talking in about five minutes. She had a quick sip of a milkshake she was drinking through a straw, before turning back to the tablet device she was talking to her mother on.

"These Chinese communists are telling me random shit every day! Like, more and more rules, none of which make any sense... It's all a fucking psy-op, this whole virus and all, which was cooked up in some commie lab here in Wuhan by the way... And we don't know how much these Chinese fuckers are spying on our communications, either!"

"Hey, don't swear so much and just calm down, sweetheart. I need you to slow down, focus and tell me about your passport issue, please."

Emma sighed at her mother's insistence for good manners at a time like this.

"The bastards say I gotta get a new passport from the US Embassy in Beijing... But then I can't fly out until Wuhan's quarantine ends, and there are no postal deliveries being allowed into Hubei. So it's all a big, fat fucking Catch 22, which I'm sure they love... Y'know, mentally torturing an American girl!"

Emma glanced at her phone and was distracted by a local news article. Written in Mandarin, the article was about the current date in the Chinese calendar. A thought occurred to her as she turned back to look at her mother on her screen's tablet. "You know, I should've thought about the Chinese New Year!"

"Why's that, honey?"

"Because it's the Year of the Rat in their calendar," Emma replied. "So what if we are now being viewed as rats by the Global Elite? I might start researching what sewer rats have to do to survive... Study what special skills they have, as I may need them!"

"Forget about all the paranoia, Emma... Because there's something I need to tell you."

"It's time we Americans put aside our dislike of Trump's personality," Emma said, clearly not listening to her mom. "Which is a reaction I think we all have, as he's an obvious narcissist... and instead focus on his policies."

"Emma, listen–"

"The fact is Trump is trying to prevent a Radical Leftist machine that has wormed its way into America and will go to any extreme to get power. Trump is the only one trying to keep America open and not in lockdown... Nor does he want everyone wearing masks all the time... He's trying to resist the tyrannical, anti-freedom policies being implemented here in China and throughout much of the rest of the world in the name of the virus... He knows it's all a plandemic and a scamdemic!"

Heather could see Emma wasn't going to stop. When her daughter got on these conspiratorial rants in support of

Trump, such lectures often lasted minutes at a time and led to her becoming irate.

"The fact that Trump is resisting that evil prick Bill Gates and his World Health Organization's malicious agenda to keep us enslaved forever in–"

"I have leukaemia!" Heather finally exploded.

Emma went quiet immediately. It took her a full ten seconds to digest what her mother had just said.

"I have been having some tests recently as I felt unwell. This morning, both my biopsy and Complete Blood Count results came back... "

Emma felt as if a knife was repeatedly stabbing her in the stomach as she listened to her mother reveal that a medical report showed she had an advanced form of leukaemia.

When her mother also mentioned that doctors were only giving her a few weeks left to live, Emma felt the room she was in was spinning. Almost as if she was experiencing an earthquake.

The totally unexpected news made Emma slowly begin to break down. She slumped down in her wooden chair and felt herself mentally contracting. She looked at her mother and suddenly felt guilty she had been so argumentative lately and only worried about her own issues.

Emma tried to speak, but her throat felt strangulated. No words could come out. She could only listen as her mother went on to explain in a slightly apologetic tone that she'd been feeling ill for some time but didn't want to worry her.

The last thing Heather revealed was that she'd decided to attempt to treat her condition naturally, via alternative therapies.

This final bit of bad news gave Emma her voice back. She sat bolt upright in her chair again and moved her head close to the webcam on her tablet device.

"Mom, you need to be in hospital to access specialist treatment!" Emma said, sounding hysterical. "You've always been a wonder woman, but this is one thing you cannot fix alone!"

"This is the most advanced leukaemia, like I said... So I'd need aggressive chemo... But all such treatments are being delayed due to COVID-19 patients taking priority. And you know me, I believe in alternative medicine anyway."

"But Mom, you can't give up!"

"Who said anything about giving up? I'm going to fight it, but my own way."

"I understand, Mom! But I need you to promise me that you'll at least consider conventional treatments?"

Heather looked at her daughter seriously. She eventually nodded.

"Okay... I will think on it, for you."

11

..-. .- -.-. . ..--- ..-. .- -.-. .

LONDON, UK / BALI, INDONESIA

"**G**IVEN THAT I have a pregnant wife," Mark said, "you know, the one you've never met… "

The two long-lost brothers – Mark, in London, and Elijah, in Bali – were once more communicating on a video call. As before, Mark was doing all the talking. Their previous chat had been cut short when Mark had received a late-night text from a concerned employee in his events management company.

Mark continued, "And a business that's facing bankruptcy in this bloody economic meltdown... Then, if you were a normal brother, I wouldn't hesitate to allow you to adopt Sophie."

As Mark ranted to his baby bro about all his shortcomings, Elijah just listened. Mark was confused by Elijah's silence as he'd always known him to be combative and argumentative. In fact, he normally had to fight to get a word in or to make a point. It had always been that way – even when growing up on the Broads in the English county of Norfolk, in East Anglia, although back then Elijah never caused any problems and the brothers were close.

It was almost lunchtime in London. Mark looked away from his sibling on screen as a bird caught his attention outside. It flew up onto the windowsill outside his office.

Since being forced to work from home as a result of the continuing COVID-19 lockdown, he'd noticed birds were frequent visitors to the window ledge outside his office. He attributed this to the fact that the branches of a large sycamore tree reached all the way up to and beyond the fourth floor of the South Kensington apartment building he called home.

Given he had been forced to spend so much time indoors since Britain's lockdown began, he often found himself daydreaming out the window at the big, old, healthy-looking tree.

Mark knew nothing about trees, but he almost felt like he and that tree had somehow gotten to know each other a little over recent weeks. Even though he had a wife and young niece living with him, he felt some kind of a connection to this tree.

I must be losing my marbles!

The sun burst through the clouds at that moment. It shone onto the leaves of the tree and created a magical light versus shade effect. Some of the sunlight broke through gaps in the leaves and branches to lower levels of the tree near Mark's windowsill.

A large, blue butterfly was suddenly illuminated in the sunlight outside. It was resting on one of the leaves. Mark thought it was one of the largest, most beautiful butterflies he had ever seen in his life.

The howl of a nearby siren carried to him. He looked through the branches of the sycamore tree in time to see an ambulance speeding toward Knightsbridge along nearby Old Brompton Road. As the noise faded into the distance, he returned his attention to the butterfly only to discover it had flown off.

Disappointed, Mark returned his gaze back to Elijah on his desktop computer monitor and sighed. His brother was one headache too many at this point in his life. Not only that: Elijah had destroyed his relationship with his family as far as he was concerned.

All the past sprung forth in Mark's mind and he suddenly found himself reminding Elijah about everything he'd done wrong in his life. It was a long list of fuck-ups.

At one point Elijah went to defend himself, but Mark cut him off before he could utter more than a word.

Mark reminded his brother how he'd had to bail him out so many times during his twenties. That had included sending money to him as well as writing letters to law enforcement officers and debt collectors.

Elijah allowed his brother to talk, or rant, until he finally ran out of steam. "Well," he said in the ensuing silence, "what if all that's no longer me?"

Mark was pissed that his brother seemed so calm. He noticed Elijah appeared to be living in a beach house of sorts overlooking the sea in Bali. It looked like paradise, and that didn't improve his mood any.

You probably have low blood pressure, you little prick! And you're super relaxed as you never had to take any responsibility like a real man.

Mark studied Elijah's face as he thought more about him.

You never have faced anything head on like I have. You just run away from things, adventuring around the world to please yourself!

"What if that person you're describing is now someone else?" Elijah asked.

"Tough shit," Mark replied. "You've poisoned the well by abusing our trust once too often. That's why your own sister stopped contacting you. That's why our mother and father didn't even leave you anything in their will!"

"I was never worried about their money, Mark. I knew you and Vicky deserved whatever little they had left. I never asked for any of it."

Mark ignored Elijah's conciliatory tone. "So here's the bottom line, Elijah. While you continue gallivanting around the world, Sophie has been orphaned... And you've never shown anything that tells me I can trust you with the responsibility of looking after a six year old girl."

"You really think I would neglect my own niece?"

Mark shook his head. He laughed as if to tell his younger brother that he thought he was an absolute joke.

Elijah didn't react. His gaze was unwaveringly unblinking. It conveyed that he meant everything he'd said and implied about evolving as a person.

12

..-. .- -.-. . ..--- ..-. .- -.-. .

WEST BANK, PALESTINE | RIO DE JANEIRO, BRAZIL

I N AIDA REFUGEE Camp, Mariam had not found any new employment yet, but she had a respectable job interview lined up at least. It would be held the following week at an office for the UNRWA, or the United Nations Relief and Works Agency.

Although the camp contained no health clinics, the UNRWA provided limited financial assistance for Palestinian physicians to offer some basic medical treatments within the camp.

Mariam was praying she'd get the job, even though she didn't fully trust the UNRWA. Although the UN managed the agency specifically to provide relief for Palestinian refugees, she couldn't see what it had done for her people in the seventy-one years of its existence.

However, she also knew beggars couldn't be choosers in her precarious situation as an unemployed single mother during a global pandemic. About half of Aida's working-age adults were unemployed at any given time, but due to Coronavirus restrictions over three-quarters of the camp's residents were now jobless.

Mariam sat down in the lounge of the apartment she and her son lived in. Her son was outside the camp with his tennis coach, and the elderly grandmother of one of the three other refugee families they shared the apartment with was home.

This was extremely rare alone time, or close to alone time, for Mariam. She sat before her old laptop computer and waited to connect to a video calling app. The power had failed minutes earlier and had only just come back on. She was steeling herself to call her friend, or former friend, in Rio de Janeiro.

Why do you not leave me alone Hanan? Mariam thought to herself. *Have you not caused me enough misery already?*

After their last fiery conversation, Hanan had convinced Mariam to agree to another video chat. Mariam had at first said no, but then reluctantly changed her mind and agreed to speak to her fellow Palestinian – on the proviso that it would be the final call between them.

Her painfully slow internet service finally connected to the video communication app and she was able to call Hanan.

When Hanan appeared, she could be seen moving around a noisy supermarket in Rio de Janeiro. She immediately apologized, saying she had not expected Mariam to be available to talk for another hour or so.

Mariam didn't care about that. She quickly reiterated she wanted this to be their final call and that she still saw no valid reason why they should waste their time communicating.

"There are still very important things I need to tell you," Hanan began. She paused as she bumped into a toddler in one of the supermarket's aisles. After profusely apologizing in fluent Portuguese to the child's mother, she returned her attention to the video call. "And I totally get that you hate me, Mariam," Hanan said, reverting to Arabic. "And I believe I deserve that hate. So after I say what I need to say, I'll understand if you never talk to me again... Which is perfectly fine."

Hanan went on to reveal more of what had happened to her in the intervening years since Mariam had last seen her. How she dated Mariam's ex-fiancé Michael after he left Mariam for her. How she and Michael had lived together and how they'd split several years later after he cheated on her.

"Cheaters never change," Hanan said.

"I still don't care about any of this," Mariam protested.

Hanan persisted with her story, describing how she became a fully qualified architect in a Rio university and eventually helped design some of the most impressive new buildings in all of Latin America.

This especially touched a nerve with Mariam because before becoming pregnant, while still engaged to Michael, she had begun studying to be an architect herself. That had been her dream also. And given they had once been best friends, Mariam knew that Hanan remembered all this.

Hanan carried on talking about her life experiences and mentioned how wealthy the architecture firm was that she worked for.

That was the final straw for Mariam and she snapped. "So great, you're rich and successful and I'm not. Is that what you wanted to tell me? That you became the sort of architect I should have also become? You want to rub salt in my wounds, is that it?"

"No, on the contrary! With the world coming to a standstill this year, all these things I worked so hard for, just suddenly... mean nothing to me. That is what I am trying to tell you, Mariam. That I now realize all that matters is who I am inside... And this is why I need to deal with what I did to you."

Mariam shook her head. "It's far too late and the permanent damage was done long ago. You did what you did to me and I suffered as a result. End of story."

Hanan was about to say something she felt sure would prove her old friend wrong when the sound of an opening door was heard at Mariam's end. Hanan saw Mariam turn away for a moment then look back sharply at into her web-cam.

"My son's home from his tennis practice," Mariam said. "I must go. So please, that's it between us now. Just leave me alone."

As Mariam terminated the call, Hanan felt infuriated. She wanted to scream out in rage right there in the supermarket, but restrained herself.

Hanan wasn't angry with Mariam at all. She was upset with herself for not cutting to the chase earlier in the conversation and telling Mariam what she'd really wanted to say.

13

..-. .- -.-. . ..--- ..-. .- -.-. .

ZÜRICH, SWITZERLAND | AUCKLAND, NEW ZEALAND

SEEING BYRON'S CONCERNED face made Albert's stomach churn. The last thing he wanted to do was cause any further pain.

Seated in his luxurious home office in Zürich, Albert had just spent the last few minutes trying to assure the New Zealander that his intentions were good. In a way, he regretted he hadn't at least hinted at the nature of his revelations before their live podcast began. On the other hand, he still felt his more mysterious approach was somehow the right way to go about it.

As a tense-looking Byron prepared to ask his next question, Albert thought about his own motivations.

He tried to simplify in his mind what he really wanted to say to Byron and the international audience the Kiwi referred to as Undergrounders.

How to reveal how the world's powers-that-be really operate without confusing regular folk?

Besides all the little-known facts he was about to disclose, the Ghanaian also wanted to get across the complex dangers of modern media. In particular, how it shaped people's minds without them realizing it.

At the elite levels of power Albert had operated at throughout most of his working life, he'd observed that the key to controlling the planet could be summarized in one word: *Narrative.*

Whoever was truly in power – not the obvious political power but the puppet masters pulling the strings above that – would always tell convincing yet often deceptive narratives. They did this via storytelling in the news media, entertainment media, social media and other outlets they owned and managed.

Albert also knew that studies had shown many people could easily recall stories they had read or heard years or decades ago, but often could not recall important facts they had come across only a minutes before. Furthermore, he knew many memory techniques involved creating a story to go along with the information that one wanted to recall – additional proof for him that *story* was inherent in the way the human mind worked and was the primary basis for memory retention.

Whether it was stories about the financial system, or wars, or oil shortages, the storytelling would always rely on one thing. And that was a certain emotion that needed to be evoked within the news stories or narratives. It was a proven way to have a more powerful, long-lasting effect on the minds of the masses. And this crucial emotion always related to survival needs.

Concepts about survival nearly always produced fear, and fear triggered the reptilian brain, and the reptilian brain activated the fight or flight emotional response in humans. The extreme fight or flight state, Albert knew, was always so vivid to humans that it would lock in the overarching narratives.

Anyone trapped in the survival mode would listen to and believe whatever they thought was in their best interests to survive. Albert also knew from direct experience that this was one reason why the elites who controlled the Earth did not want too many people becoming financially free or getting beyond this constant survival mode.

Albert passionately believed that malaise was what society most needed a cure for.

It's time to get people out of survival mode programming.

He felt sure the more people who could be pulled out of that mode, the better off humanity would be.

"So what's your purpose in appearing on this episode of Underground Knowledge, Albert?" Byron's slightly irritated voice snapped Albert out of his own thoughts. "To remind me of my past?"

"No. This is a live confession," Albert replied. "To disclose before your audience, and the world, the terrible thing I did to you... And then try to make amends."

"The terrible thing you did to me? But we've never met before today."

Albert shook his head to indicate things were slightly more complicated than that.

Over the next few minutes, he revealed he was formerly one of the aforementioned "financial overlords" at the helm of the invisible economy. An economy, he said, that was worth quadrillions of dollars.

Byron immediately understood Albert was the very type of person he had been trying to expose in the newspaper article he had written at the Sydney Morning Herald. That type being some kind of bankster or other high finance shark who was a true enemy of the common people.

Next, Albert confessed something even more shocking – that he was the grand architect who had gotten Byron fired from his print journalism position at that same newspaper.

Byron couldn't believe what he was hearing. He blinked several times as he tried to make sense of what he'd just heard. As his thinking clarified, he became incensed.

"Do you have any idea how much pain your actions have caused me?"

"Yes," Albert said. "I know perfectly well, Byron. In fact, I have researched everything about your –"

"No, I don't think you do know. I lost my fiancé and my career, and my mother died believing I was an insane, paranoid conspiracy theorist!"

As Byron stared at the older man before him on his computer screen, he could feel tears threatening as he thought of his recently deceased mother.

14

..-. .- -.-. . ..--- ..-. .- -.-. .

JERUSALEM, ISRAEL | SYDNEY, AUSTRALIA

ESTHER CLASPED A handful of reddish soil as she bathed in the gentle, early-morning sunshine in the communal backyard of her apartment building in Jerusalem. Letting the dirt trickle slowly through her fingers and onto the sunbaked earth below, she looked into the camera lens of the phone she held in her other hand.

The Israeli was still communicating with Levi down at the bottom of the world in Sydney. Levi was in a relaxed state in the lounge of his apartment where darkness was chasing the last of the daylight away.

The pair had been talking for hours on the same chat that had begun with Levi walking around Sydney's Eastern Suburbs and on Coogee Beach. They'd had a short break when Levi's return to his apartment complex coincided with an elderly female neighbor needing his help with some urgent building maintenance.

As a result of their lengthy video chat, Esther hadn't slept at all during the night. That didn't bother her however as she had lost track of time lately during Israel's Covid lockdown which had prevented her working or even going out much.

For some reason she often slept during the day and stayed up all night.

A blue butterfly suddenly landed on the top of Esther's phone, covering her camera and half of the screen as well. She was amazed by its color and sheer size. The vivid blue patterns on its outstretched wings looked splendid against the Earth's red dirt below the phone.

Esther reached out to touch the butterfly, but it flapped its wings and flew away before she could make contact.

She returned her attention to Levi. He'd been subtly conveying that he was ready to settle down. He hadn't exactly said he felt she might be the one for him, but she suspected he was building to that.

"I'm damaged beyond repair, Levi," Esther said, as if to stop him in his tracks. "So even if we met again, I wouldn't be the right woman for you. I'm like the glass that breaks into a thousand pieces under a synagogue's chuppah at a wedding."

She glanced around her building's backyard and her neighbourhood of Neve Granot as she considered her life.

After a minute or so, she looked back at Levi's face on her phone's screen.

"Since you knew me, all those years ago... I've been shattered... And now I don't know how to put myself back together again."

Over the next few minutes, by offering a listening ear and asking insightful and respectful questions, Levi managed to help Esther open up to him even further.

She revealed to him that she'd been badly abused by two different men she'd dated in recent years. And that in her assessment that was the primary reason she now suffered depression.

Levi was also surprised to learn she had even felt suicidal on occasion.

Esther could sense he felt genuine empathy for her. He looked extremely sad for what had happened to her since they had last seen each other.

Once Esther had finished revealing the painful experiences of her life, Levi decided he should also talk about his own problems.

"I've realized I'm just a scared man on the inside, Esther. I'm scared of dying, scared of being trapped in a life I don't want to live, scared of being a pathetic nobody."

Levi thought deeply about himself for a moment. Esther remained respectfully silent as she waited for him to formulate his thoughts. "My father died when I was twenty-nine."

"I'm sorry," Esther said. "I didn't even know he had passed."

"Thank you. He always liked you, you know?"

Esther smiled compassionately at him.

"Anyway, I realized in hindsight I never fully respected my dad. I mean, I did have respect for him, but not to the level I should have. I guess I judged him from the perspective of all the things a young man usually cares about... "

Levi thought back to some uncomfortable memories he had of his father. Or more specifically, memories of the way he interacted with his father.

"He wasn't that good at making money. I mean, he always provided for my mother and our family, but that was it. He never looked to make more than survival money. Sure my father provided enough to live on, but that wasn't enough for me. I'd always compare him to my friends' wealthy parents and feel disappointment and let down. I loved my father, but at times felt ashamed of him."

"I see," Esther said.

"But then eventually, as I got older, I realized none of that shit truly matters. All that's left now is the memory that my dad loved my mother, would do anything for her. And that he always made his family his number one priority... And probably the most important thing was he taught us to all feel our own self-worth. Which as you know, for us Jews, with so much anti-Semitism in the world, with virtually everyone hating us or blaming us, we must have tremendous self-worth or else we are truly nothing. And my dad gave us that in spades."

Esther nodded understandingly.

"You know," Levi continued, "now that I'm much older and have more life experience... I look back at what I had back then and I can't help but conclude that I was the richest poor kid. My home always consisted of love, affection, support, unity and most of all good principles. I really had everything! The irony was that it was all of my wealthy friends were some of the loneliest people on the planet. They may have had all the materials in the world but at the end of the day they're just materials. Despite all their wealth, their lives contained no substance. Only a house full of emptiness... Now I realize what's important. It's not about building the best house, it's about building the best home. Creating a safe environment. Making sure everyone feels loved, safe, and has an abundance of self-worth... So I guess what I am now afraid of, more than anything, is never finding or creating the same sort of home."

Levi was aware the flood gates were really opening up now.

Damn, you're rambling, you bloody dickhead!

He couldn't seem to stop himself though and for some reason just wanted to tell Esther, more than anyone else in the world, everything he'd come to understand about himself during the isolation of the lockdown.

Cut to the chase, mate!

"I imagine...you're probably wondering what made me think of you after all of these years, right?"

Esther didn't acknowledge the question. She was feeling somewhat hesitant – unsure where all this was going.

"To be honest I'm not exactly sure myself, Esther. But one thing I do know is that you've always had strong family values. Even when we dated you always respected your parents as not once did you ever fail to make curfew. You truly loved your family as you should. And realizing that I overlooked the wonderful family who raised me is what made me think of you again, I feel."

Get to the point, you stupid idiot!

Levi cleared his throat as he finally got to the point he'd been trying to make to Esther for days now.

"So I know this may sound crazy, and I know I'm eighteen years too late, but I just wanted to tell you that you're the only girl I ever truly... I dunno, I guess I was just wondering... If you may–"

"I don't feel the same thing here," Esther interjected, "if that's what you're asking?"

Levi looked at her on his tablet's screen. He realized he was once more witnessing a colder, harder side to her personality. The Aussie noticed she even seemed slightly amused by the fact that whatever he was suggesting might still exist.

"I mean," Esther continued, "we were basically kids way back then, right? 2020 might be driving us all insane or delusional, I know... But we can't slip back into juvenile fantasies that will lead us nowhere."

Levi attempted to hide the fact that he felt a little crestfallen as he continued to stare at Esther on his tablet. He also tried to reconcile the tougher exterior she was exhibiting with the softer, more angelic young lady he'd once fallen in love with.

Just then an email notification message popped up at the top right hand corner of Levi's tablet device. He was very surprised to see who the email's sender was.

Ayanda.

Levi lost his concentration for a moment.

Ayanda was one person he had not thought about in a long while and just seeing her name immediately triggered an automatic physical response.

15

WUHAN, CHINA / HOUSTON, USA

EMMA HAD INDIGESTION. Having not long returned home after an evening of shopping for groceries, she'd removed her compulsory mask and gloves and had scoffed down a home-cooked meal, which comprised a packet of instant noodles.

The shopping expedition had taken much longer than expected as the store she usually frequented near her aparthotel had been raided by Chinese authorities – "on suspicion of management breaking Coronavirus regulations," she'd been told by a Mandarin-speaking store manager.

It had turned out to be a false alarm and the store had done nothing wrong. Nevertheless, it had delayed Emma. A large queue had formed outside the facility as the store's management was only allowed to let in so many customers per hour.

Coronavirus protocols like this were all part of the ultra-strict, regimented lockdown the Chinese Communist Party were enforcing. Almost any public activities besides shopping – especially something as unnecessary as the video call Emma wanted to make – were illegal until further notice.

This had almost screwed up Emma's plans as she had organized to speak with her mother at breakfast time in Houston – before Heather's scheduled appointment with her general practitioner at the local medical center.

She just managed to make it home in time, but panicked when she saw her mom's profile icon on the video app they used indicated she was offline. In fact, her status was revealed to be *unavailable*. Emma only calmed down when she discovered her mother had also sent her a message on another communication app to say she'd decided to leave earlier than indicated to avoid delays in the commute to downtown Houston.

Later that evening in Wuhan, Emma was finally in direct contact with Heather as she was being driven home by cab following her downtown doctor's appointment. Looking at her beautiful, radiant mom, Emma found it hard to believe the woman she observed on her laptop screen had advanced leukaemia. Her brain just couldn't compute that.

Emma's thoughts were interrupted when she observed some kind of commotion occurring outside of Heather's cab. There was lots of shouting. "What's happening there, mom?" Her concern heightened when she saw the alarm on her mother's face.

"I'm not sure," Heather said. "It looks like some kind of protest."

"A protest? For what?"

Heather tensed when someone banged a placard against the cab's front windscreen, prompting the cabbie to curse and sound the cab's horn. The placard's sign read: FEAR IS THE REAL VIRUS. It was one of a dozen such placards being paraded by anti-Coronavirus lockdown protestors.

Returning her attention to Emma on her phone's screen, Heather said, "It's a protest against the lockdowns by the looks."

Emma was pleasantly surprised there was resistance to lockdowns in Texas, especially as Coronavirus restrictions had not been in force in America as long as in China.

"Here, let me show you, sweetheart," Heather said.

As her mother turned her phone's camera to the cab's rear passenger side window and filmed the protestors, Emma was amazed. She felt it was some kind of validation of the American spirit that she was witnessing. There were twenty protestors at most, but she assumed this was just the beginning and more would soon protest at what she felt sure was global tyranny.

Emma was fairly certain the virus was real and required a response from the authorities. However, she resonated with President Trump's stance. Especially his insistence that the "cure" must not be "worse than the problem itself" – as well as his calls to reopen America ASAP. She didn't mention Trump, however, for she knew Heather loathed the man.

As she continued to survey the Houston protestors on her screen, she marveled at their display of resistance. Many in the group appeared to be mothers. They held signs like "Protect Future Freedoms of Our Children" and similar pro-liberty signs, including ones that quoted basic freedoms expressed in the US Constitution.

Emma felt encouraged because it had only been several weeks earlier that anyone criticizing the lockdowns or other anti-virus measures had been labeled a complete nutcase. She did, however, fear that a pro-lockdown versus anti-lockdown scenario might soon emerge in society. And she wondered whether the global elites had factored that polarity into their projections.

The bastards at the top really know how to create divide-and-conquer situations!

She also prayed that what was happening in China would not be rolled out internationally. Especially not back home in the States. Already, she'd observed, there appeared to be zero consideration for human rights, privacy or individual freedoms in the Chinese government's response to the perceived COVID-19 threat.

None of that shit matters now anyway!

Emma no longer cared for any of these conspiracies and she even felt no real emotion toward what she deemed human rights violations. This despite the fact that only twenty-four hours earlier her mind had basically been possessed by Coronavirus conspiracies and she had been ranting online about them most of her waking hours.

All that mattered now was one thing.

My mom.

As Heather's cabbie left the Houston protestors in his rearview mirror, Emma refocused on her mother. "What have you decided, Mom?" she asked.

"Hang on," Heather said. "I'll tell you when I get home, sweetheart."

Emma agreed to call her back a little later.

"I spoke to Doctor Johns about my diagnosis," Heather said, "and the leukaemia is too far advanced. I'm sorry."

Heather was back in her apartment in downtown Houston.

It was now fairly late in Wuhan. Fortunately, Emma was a night owl and often at her best around midnight or even after. Her mind was therefore focused and she was processing everything she was hearing at speed.

"There's nothing much mainstream medicine can do for me anyway. Besides, hospitals are filling up with patients infected with COVID-19... So if I catch this virus, it'll finish me off."

Unlike her daughter, Heather believed the virus issue was a serious threat and supported the lockdown policies. And she thought Trump's approach was irresponsible and would lead to disaster.

"I can't let you give up, Mom!"

"Who said anything about giving up? Mainstream medicine is only one pathway. So, I'm going to try the power of the mind and alternative health remedies instead."

"But you must fight for life."

"You're not listening to me, Emma. I told you I'm going to fight for life. People have defeated leukaemia solely through alternative therapies. So, please, just trust me, I'm going to find a way to survive."

Heather hesitated as she looked at her daughter on her screen.

"But, sweetheart, just in case... Well, let's say, for the sake of argument, I don't have much time... We don't know what the future will hold, right? So I need to tell you everything I was planning to share with you in the next few years of your life..."

Emma grew even more devastated as the gravity of the moment sunk in.

"As you journey further into your womanhood, I need to tell you everything I know right now. In case I am not around to..."

Heather couldn't bring herself to finish the sentence. She felt sick to her stomach knowing that she might not be around to see Emma grow and evolve and eventually perhaps marry and have kids of her own. She didn't so much feel sad that she herself may die. Rather, her fear was for Emma being totally alone and having nobody to guide her should she have to face the various curveballs that life invariably threw everyone's way at some stage.

Emma's father, Heather's ex-husband, had left when their daughter was only three. Heather didn't even know where he was. Her own parents had died during Emma's formative years so there was literally nobody else to turn to.

Heather began to reveal to her daughter a few of the more important life experiences she'd had. These included very adult experiences with men.

Tired, Heather prepared to say goodbye to Emma for the day – or goodnight in her daughter's case.

"Remember, my child," she said. "You may be far from eyes… "

Emma knew this saying. It was something her mother had always recited whenever one or other of them went their separate ways, even if only for a day or two. She found herself having to fight hard not to cry as she saw her mother placing one hand over her heart.

"But you'll always be close to my heart," Heather said.

In keeping with the ritual they always observed, mother and daughter kissed their own fingers then placed them over the web-cam lenses as if to touch each other. It was their way of saying goodbye.

On this occasion, however, the ritual had heightened meaning for them both. Each was acutely aware this really could be *goodbye*.

16

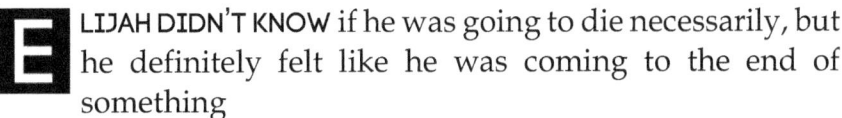

BALI, INDONESIA / LONDON, UK

ELIJAH DIDN'T KNOW if he was going to die necessarily, but he definitely felt like he was coming to the end of something

The end of what exactly?

He hoped it was just the end of a life cycle and the beginning of something new, much like a caterpillar evolving into a butterfly.

Regardless, after many years of exploring the world and living a nomadic lifestyle, Elijah had suddenly, and perhaps finally, extinguished the desire to visit more new places. In fact, he somehow knew Bali's Kuta Beach, where he'd been for many months now, would be the last foreign destination he'd visit anytime soon. Whether that meant he was about to die, he still did not know. Since leaving England in his early twenties, Elijah had worked his way around the world and had many adventures on the road.

He'd started out moving around the European Union, working as a laborer mostly in warehouses. Then he'd gone further abroad to Commonwealth countries – former British Empire colonies like Canada, New Zealand and Australia where, as a UK citizen, he was allowed to live and work for one year at a time.

During his time Down Under, he worked in animal recovery shelters, and connected so much with animals he soon became a vegan. He had decided that killing a conscious, intelligent being, or supporting the killing of an animal, just to fill his belly, was something he could never do again.

Around this time he also began to experience an intense loneliness. Even when surrounded by friends or in relationships with women, that sad, intense feeling was always there, buried deep inside. Consequently, he'd begun to feel separated from others and dissatisfied with the very things that pleased them.

Every few years or so he returned home to England, but never staying for long and always wanting to leave.

He had come to understand that he'd been running from something in his past, or more likely running from his flawed character, for that's how he viewed it, or from his personality. And the loneliness remained with him, too, like a curse within.

Elijah felt it was these feelings that eventually drove him to seek out more exotic locations such as Thailand, Nepal, Vietnam and India. And it was in those locations that he first began to meditate and become a true spiritual seeker.

To fund his travels in the Far East he worked, sometimes with a work permit and sometimes without one, as an English teacher or else he would volunteer to work for charities in exchange for food and accommodation.

In more recent times he'd shifted into online work as a freelancer to facilitate a digital nomad lifestyle. This had organically morphed into a writing career simply because he'd ended up writing so many blogs and articles. His writing improved rapidly and he was surprised that he had a very strong voice that came through in all the written work he posted online.

One spin-off to come out of his paid online writing was he attracted followers seeking guidance or spiritual wisdom. Or something. He had no name for whatever it was they were after. The truth was he'd never sought to be a spiritual teacher, yet he was aware that was exactly what he had become. Nor did he ever charge money for spiritual advice. He just freely shared whatever insights he had about life and people, and about the unique and sometimes distressing situations individuals found themselves in.

Fellow travelers – many of them backpackers and often confused souls as he had once been – invariably wanted to keep in touch with him after they went their separate ways, and his online platform enabled them to do that no matter where in the world they were. Elijah's reach wasn't limited to backpackers and other travelers; stay-at-homers also reached out to him. This was his motivation to host free meditation sessions most days via video conferences with his followers, such was his growing popularity.

In the last year or so, he had also started writing a mystical non-fiction book he believed offered practical techniques that could revolutionize readers' lives. These included secrets he had learned from yogis and yoginis, and from other wise men and women, in the Himalayas of India and Nepal.

To his surprise, the book had not only secured him representation by a respected London literary agent, but a major UK publishing house had just submitted an offer to publish it.

Later that day, Elijah was hiking through one of Bali's rainforests in the middle of the island. He was once again talking to his older brother, Mark, who was in a suit and tie and was walking through the congested streets of the world's premiere financial district, the City of London.

Mark was on his way home from an important meeting with a financier. The meeting had not gone well. In fact, the financier had said no to his refinancing request and now his events management company was looking like it might go under.

The only good news was that the United Kingdom's Prime Minister, Boris Johnson, had indicated Britain's COVID-19 lockdown may soon end. Mark was hoping that was the case and that somehow live events would soon resume so his business could continue as before.

Looking at his cell phone screen, Mark shook his head as he watched his long-haired, bearded, younger brother ambling through the rainforest in Bali, looking as if he didn't have a care in the world. A puff of wind gently ruffled Elijah's hair.

Lazy bugger.

"You're thirty-five years old," Mark said into his phone. "Yet, you're still a bloody kid! So how could you possibly look after a girl as young as Sophie?"

Elijah sighed then smiled.

My, my, what a tangled web we weave.

How ironic it was, Elijah thought to himself, that he could so easily advise his spiritual followers how to rectify mistakes in their own lives, or deal with the past – and yet in his own life it was so difficult to know what to do.

In another way, however, that made perfect sense to him. When advising others it was possible to be objective, but with one's own life objectivity was virtually impossible. Humans often could not see the wood for the trees with their own lives, he figured. Somehow they had to grope in the dark, trying to figure out the best moves to make by an agonizing trial and error process.

Still, Elijah believed the recent tumultuous events in his family back in England presented an opportunity. He felt the universe was offering him a chance for redemption.

If only my brother will give me another chance.

"There's this thing that happens when you're sailing," he said at length.

Mark thought his brother was cracking up. "Sailing?"

"Yeah. So in those yacht races, you know like the America's Cup and shit like that, you can go dead straight to the finish line, right?"

"O... kay."

"And that would make perfect sense," Elijah said, "as it's the quickest way from A to B. However, there's another maneuver you can do in sailing which is called tacking. That's when you take a big risk, sailing way off course."

Mark paused for a moment in the busy City of London pedestrian traffic. Given all he was going through in his personal and business life, and given the diabolical state of the world with the global pandemic and everything else, he couldn't believe his brother was rambling about nothing.

Who gives a flying fuck about sailing at a time like this?

"But sometimes," Elijah said, "what happens with sailing is a yacht that tacks off course, departing from the obvious path to the finish line, finds a useful breeze that pushes it ahead of its competitors." Puffing as he scrambled over a fallen log, he added, "It now has major momentum and can win the race."

As Elijah headed deeper into the Balinese rainforest, and Mark walked along Fleet Street toward Blackfriars train station, there was a drawn-out silence between them. Mark didn't quite understand whatever Elijah was alluding to, but he was suddenly ready to listen and stop interrupting with sarcastic jibes.

Elijah didn't know if it was just because his brother was tired or what, but he decided to take advantage of the silence. He spent the next few minutes talking about his travels. Even though Mark was not religious or spiritual and was more of an agnostic, Elijah decided to open up about the profound experiences he'd had off the beaten track – in the Far East and other places. He described having epiphanies in the jungles of South East Asia and on the mountain tops in the Himalayas, and how something gradually changed inside him. He explained how at long last he really had matured and become wiser, and, more importantly, how he'd had profound spiritual realizations about the reality of life.

"I found my true self, Mark," he said. "Something different to my former self that I didn't like – and I know you certainly never liked either. And those powerful revelations also killed my ego… Killed the previous resistance I had to submitting to God's will… Killed that side of me that wanted to argue with others and always be rebellious and selfishly so."

Mark paused outside Blackfriars underground train station. He continued to listen to Elijah as he studied a noticeboard at the underground entrance.

"So coming back to the sailing analogy," Elijah said. "That's what happened. I got blown way off course. I lost my way, Mark, I'll admit. But ultimately, I found something extraordinary. And now I'm heading home, and back to the Light, with momentum. The wind is in my sails now. I know I am capable of adopting Sophie and raising her as a loving father would."

A somewhat bemused Mark received a text message on his phone. It was from the financier he'd just met. The message indicated the financier wanted to talk. Mark returned his attention to Elijah on the continuing video chat. He knew he needed to wrap up the call, but before he did he wanted to quickly figure out what the hell his brother was getting at.

"So what're you saying, Elijah? That you found God and ended up singing Kumbaya with the locals in a Thai jungle or on some Indian mountaintop?"

"No. Well, kinda. But more importantly, I saw all the errors of my ways. I saw how I'd hurt you. I remember how I hurt our parents and disrespected our family… And I'm sorry."

17

AUCKLAND, NEW ZEALAND / ZÜRICH, SWITZERLAND

AS THE LIVE Underground Knowledge podcast continued, Byron still felt ready to explode.

He wanted to tell Albert he was the most evil son-of-a-bitch who ever existed for getting him fired from the Sydney Morning Herald two years earlier. He wanted all of his audience to know exactly what an asshole Albert was.

At the same time, however, he hadn't yet established what Albert's motivations were. The Zürich-based African remained infuriatingly poker-faced.

Frustrated, Byron took a deep breath and glanced out his window for a moment at Auckland's harbor suburb of Devonport. He decided to be as direct as possible with his guest. "So what are you tryin' to achieve here, Albert? Destroy me further? Take away whatever livelihood I still have left?"

"No, on the contrary I want to try to make things right."

Byron felt embarrassed he was losing his shit before a live audience. On the other hand, he didn't give a toss. He was at rock bottom anyway, and he felt like life had chipped away most of his dignity and self-respect – not to mention his ego.

Let's face it, your audience is tiny and none of them care about you!

"So how the hell are you gonna put things right now, Albert? Use a time machine?"

"No," Albert replied, calm as ever. "I am giving you a massive news story... Most of the damage I did is irreparable, I understand, but I am here to apologize... And also, on the journalistic side of the equation, it's not too late to expose the truth, son."

Byron calmed down a little as he considered what he'd just been told.

Albert continued, "Remember that investigative news story you wanted published? The one you wrote exposing the real economy? The world's true wealth? The economy behind the official economy? And remember you were like a dog with a bone?" He didn't wait for Byron to respond. "Well, because we are broadcasting live, nobody will be able to take this story away from you this time."

The older man cleared his throat, before continuing. "I was a senior figure in that invisible economy most of my life. I know for a fact there is more than enough undocumented wealth in this world for there to never be any homeless citizens... For there to be no children going hungry, or anyone to go without a proper education... and for there to never be anyone who cannot afford medical treatment."

Byron reluctantly found himself agreeing with all that.

"You ever notice how they never have enough money for basic human dignities like education, hospitals, medicine, and various other social investments? There's never enough funds left in government budgets for those things. But then... when it's for the really big stuff that suits them like trillion dollar military budgets or flying rockets into space, there's always enough money! It just somehow miraculously appears!"

Albert reached across the desk of his Zürich home office and picked up a typed document. "This is a copy of your rejected Sydney Morning Herald article I quoted from earlier… Let me read some more from it Byron as I believe you really hit the nail on the head."

Byron had no objection though he had a number of questions swirling around in his head.

Quoting from the rejected article, Albert said, "It has been purported by financial researchers and alternative media outlets that there are individuals whose net worth would dwarf whoever tops the Forbes Rich List at any given time – riches that the likes of Bill Gates, Warren Buffett or Jeff Bezos could only dream about. If this theory is true, then it would fit into a little-known financial category referred to as invisible or hidden wealth. Massive undeclared or non-disclosed fortunes virtually impossible to detect. Often derived from black market monies or Old World financial empires, it is kept stashed away in offshore tax havens or untraceable Swiss bank accounts."

Albert placed the print-out back on his desk then looked into the camera and directly addressed Byron's audience. "Some of you are probably a bit bored by economics, the financial system or even money itself. But I want to make it clear that these subjects are only monetary issues on the surface. In reality, they are humanitarian issues. Starving the masses of financial opportunities, sinking them in debt and cheating them out of various services their taxes should pay for, are among the greatest crimes those in power can ever commit. These sins result in widespread poverty, unemployment, increased crime rates, homelessness, drug addiction, overcrowded prisons and a whole host of other social problems."

Feeling Albert was running the show a little too much and remembering he had a job to do as the podcast's host, Byron quickly jumped in. "Why don't you start from the beginning, Albert? Can you explain how you got to be influential enough to get a journalist on the other side of the world silenced and fired?"

Albert nodded grimly. Reflecting on his past, he glanced out his window and briefly observed Lake Zürich and other distant landmarks in the southeastern section of the city. He then launched into an account of his life's journey and career path. His dissertation was as much for the members of Byron's audience as it was for the podcast host himself. Those members, as the host had previously advised him, were referred to as Undergrounders.

"I started out as a mining manager in my native Ghana and eventually oversaw several West African diamond mines in neighboring countries like Sierra Leone.

"During this time I came to realize diamonds were nowhere near as scarce as officially stated. They were actually fairly plentiful. However, supply was carefully controlled by the European diamond companies who owned the mines. These companies, I discovered, artificially influenced supply and demand and therefore spiked the market price of diamonds. And this created the illusion of scarcity, exactly as you stated in your newspaper article Byron."

To reinforce the point, he held up the print-out of the article that had gotten Byron fired.

Albert revealed he had taken the opposite approach taken by the former journalist. Rather than exposing the enormous financial deceptions he'd become aware of, he had instead agreed to keep everything secret so he could personally benefit.

"This ability to keep such dark secrets and lies to myself and be someone who would play the game, as they say, eventually brought me to the attention of the heavy hitters. Not heavy hitters in the mining industry, but the ones who count amongst the planet's ruling elite.

"After several promotions, I ended up helming a major diamond mining conglomerate from its headquarters in Zürich, Switzerland. From there, I became enmeshed in various elitist groups who secretly and methodically run the show. Almost inevitably, I found myself being used as an economic hit man, or a financial hyena, take your pick."

Byron didn't dare interrupt. His guest was on a roll and he sensed he had a lot more to divulge.

Albert went on to reveal he'd also discovered the global elite, or "the puppet masters" as he called them, directed world affairs via a complex network of power structures, some of which had been in place for over a millennia and dated back to the likes of the Venetian Empire and even Ancient Rome.

The fuel for these elites, he said, was primarily what he termed "Old World money". Off-the-charts wealth that had been hoarded over many centuries by Royal and aristocratic European families and mostly held in the form of gold.

"The spoils from key historical events like the rise and eventual defeat of Nazi Germany, the African slave trade, the fall of the Ancient Rome, the Crusades in the Middle East and splits in the Vatican all contributed to this immeasurable wealth. And earlier still, this Old World money dated back to the black nobility in early Europe and even as far back as Babylon some say.

"These undeclared fortunes amount to untraceable assets that no mainstream financial analyst would notice let alone comprehend."

Albert advised his audience the shadowy figures he spoke of used not only their wealth but also sophisticated networks to dominate the planet.

"One area they target is international think tanks like the Bilderberg Group, the Trilateral Commission and the Council on Foreign Relations. Another is secret societies such as Freemasonry.

"The banking sector is yet another facet of this complex, multi-layered system. Privately owned financial institutions masquerading as public entities, such as the Federal Reserve in the US and central banks in Europe, are where the financial overlords and international banksters do the bulk of the dirty work for the elites higher up in the chain."

Albert also touched on "the less-than-holy financial activities" of the Vatican Bank, and the IMF and World Bank's "less-than-charitable dealings" with the Third World.

"And like I say, I know all this as I was one of the financial overlords who facilitate such nefarious undertakings. They shape the modern world far more than politicians do. After all, money of this magnitude can buy political administrations. And money can buy elections as well, trust me!"

Byron nodded. He'd either verified or at least theorized about these revelations as an investigative journalist. Even so, it was good to get it straight from the horse's mouth.

Albert continued, "You only need to research semi-secret oaths all world leaders take to prove they have elitist affiliations and do not represent the common people."

Byron knew this for a fact. He and many of his fellow Undergrounders were also aware that many of the events that had unfolded so far in 2020 had not been organic or natural. Rather, they were mostly artificially constructed by the same global elitists his controversial guest spoke of and many world leaders had, wittingly or unwittingly, played a role in this.

"I just know that the banksters, economic hit men and financial hyenas are looking to profit or are already profiting from the unfolding Coronavirus situation," Albert said. "And worse, the likes of the World Bank and the IMF will aim to bankrupt various nations around the world during this economic meltdown."

Albert paused and reached for something off-camera, returning seconds later to face his web-cam. "I want to go beyond mere theory or hearsay on this episode with you today, Byron, because proof is what everybody needs."

To reinforce all the seemingly far-reaching concepts he was talking about he held up a bank certificate to camera, keeping it close to his computer's camera lens so Byron and the other viewers could clearly see it. It was an official certificate of account issued from a bank in Brussels, Belgium.

987 Billion USD.

Albert explained the certificate was in the name of one individual whose name he was covering with his thumb.

Byron was astonished, not just because the amount of the bank account was only 13 billion short of a trillion US dollars or because it was almost ten times more than the worth of the world's richest man, Bill Gates, as reported by Forbes and the Wall Street Journal.

What really freaked out Byron was the number itself.

987

That was the exact number that had appeared to him twice in an iridescent blue light during his out of body experiences.

Now Byron was really confused. Albert, and this entire podcast, was really starting to do his head in. His mind wandered to his recent out of body experiences. He still wondered why his life had recently taken on a mystical tone. Forgetting for the moment that he was live on the air, he recalled the blissful sensations he felt whenever he left his body.

"What I have revealed here… "

Albert's voice snapped Byron out of his daydream and back sharply to reality.

"… It reveals what I call undocumented wealth for humanity. And acknowledging it puts us on the road to breaking the spell… Breaking the lie, the illusion you wrote about, Byron, of scarcity and limited resources. And the good news is there is a reason this wealth is undocumented. It's not documented because it's all illegal, ill-gotten money stolen from the common people over time. If it were legal wealth, it would not have to be stashed away, and individuals whose net worth can be measured in the trillions and multi-trillions, or quadrillions in the case of some wealthy families and groups, would be openly acknowledged. So they hide it to disguise their crimes."

Byron noticed Albert was suddenly looking forlorn.

"I'm probably going to be killed for revealing all this today," the Ghanaian said. "But this is my karma... This is what I need to do to complete my soul's journey in this life."

18

.._-. ._- -._-. . .._--- .._-. ._- -._-. .

WEST BANK, PALESTINE / RIO DE JANEIRO, BRAZIL

MARIAM WANTED TO vomit. She could smell raw sewage. Unfortunately, this was par for the course at Aida Refugee Camp. The sewerage system was so substandard that putrid smells were common.

"Mariam? Are you okay?" Hanan asked. She was on yet another video chat with her fellow Palestinian and had noticed Mariam suddenly pulled a face.

"Just a minute," Mariam replied.

Mariam disappeared from view on Hanan's web-cam. Hanan could hear her blowing her nose.

Sitting in her office in one of several offices her architectural firm leased in a building in the financial heart of downtown Rio de Janeiro, Hanan reminded herself that she was fortunate to be self-employed. Not that she needed any reminding.

Mariam returned and resumed sitting in the room she shared with her son in the tiny West Bank refugee apartment. It had been almost three weeks since she had communicated with Hanan despite the fact her persistent Rio-based contact had been emailing her almost every day, saying there was still something very important she needed to say.

The video call had come as a surprise because Hanan never expected to hear from her former friend again, not after the way the last call ended. The irony was Mariam had placed the call by mistake. She'd meant to call another Palestinian elsewhere in the West Bank, but had somehow clicked on the wrong contact and gotten Hanan instead. Like many around the world, lockdowns were forcing her to consistently use video communications for the first time.

Regardless, Hanan had dropped everything when she saw who was calling. She was thankful to have another opportunity to share the important revelation she'd wanted to divulge all along.

"Are you alright, Mariam?"

"Ah… yes, I'm fine." Mariam debated whether to inform Hanan she'd called in error, but decided against it.

Neither spoke for a good half minute.

At length, a tentative Hanan said, "Well, I'm glad you called." She did not quite know how to begin and tried to think of something to attempt to break the ice. Eventually a subject common to them both occurred to her. "The death toll for the Coronavirus here in Brazil is skyrocketing, as you may have seen on the news… We currently have the world's highest amount of deaths and infections… And the lockdown is getting stricter… So I am very isolated here and working for weeks totally alone. That's why I am delighted to talk to you."

As Hanan continued talking, Mariam found her animosity toward her starting to fade a little. She felt like opening up a bit herself.

"I share your sentiments," Mariam said. "This year so far has been all too much for my son and I. The camp conditions are much more repressive than when you worked here. And now with these lockdowns and other virus measures, it's absolutely suffocating. If this continues, we will soon be eating out of rubbish bins!"

Mariam sighed. "If it weren't for my parents bailing us out repeatedly, we simply wouldn't have survived. But now they are sick and we cannot rely on them any longer for financial support. And now I just found out today I may have been infected by the Coronavirus! I have to get tested tomorrow. So I'm scared, I'm really scared of not being able to provide for my son anymore."

"Well, this is exactly why I wanted so badly to speak to you again," Hanan blurted out. "Because I have come into a large amount of money…and I want to gift a decent share of it to you."

Mariam was momentarily speechless.

Hanan continued, "I befriended the boss of my architectural firm… What was ironic was that he was a former Israeli citizen who had also migrated here… He was a lonely man with no family…" She hesitated as she felt herself choking up. "He died shortly before the Coronavirus outbreak and left me his entire estate… His company and his mansion house… So this is how I came to be in a position to help you out now, Mariam."

Hanan paused to wipe away a tear. Looking at Mariam, she was surprised to see her opposite didn't look happy. The unnerving, cold, expressionless stare she was now familiar with remained as cold as ever. Nothing, it seemed, had changed since they began conversing many weeks earlier.

"I would never take your money, Hanan."

"But you must! Please, I have more than enough to spare. And you are the kindest, most caring friend I ever had… And this is the only way I know how to erase some of the pain I've caused you."

"It is the past now. Like I already told you, what's done is done. So I forgive you, but I do not want to receive any of your money… Not like I am some helpless victim."

"I am not saying you are a victim. The hurt that we both feel now, the pain that I know is inside your heart, is only this intense because of the love we once both shared. You were like a big sister to me, Mariam."

Hanan was disappointed to see Mariam's cold expression and unblinking stare remained unchanged.

19

..-. .- -.-. . ..--- ..-. .- -.-. .

WUHAN, CHINA / HOUSTON, USA

A DISTRAUGHT EMMA grimaced as she stared at her mom on her tablet's slightly dusty screen. Heather looked worse for wear since they'd communicated at length just the previous day.

A lot worse for wear.

The quarantined young American wiped the dust away with a cloth in order to more clearly view her normally radiant mom. This was the first time she'd seen conclusive visual signs of her deterioration – and it came as quite a shock. Heather's once beautiful face was now pale and gaunt, and unsightly sores had formed around her mouth.

Emma closed her eyes for a moment. A part of her still couldn't believe this was happening. The dramatic deterioration in her mother's condition had happened so quickly it seemed more like a dream than real life.

More like a nightmare.

Emma was stretched out on top of the bedcovers on her bed, her tablet resting on her tummy, in the room of her Wuhan aparthotel. She found herself looking around the soulless room every so often, so painful was it to look at the woman who had delivered her into this world, the person she loved more dearly than anyone else on Earth. Every time she observed her mother, she could barely prevent herself from crying.

It took all her willpower not to reveal how stressed she felt to her mom. She'd willed herself to shed all her tears before and after each video chat they had, not during. However, she was finding that easier said than done.

I need to be strong for you Mom as together we are going to fight this and win! I will see you again. I will, I will, I will! I love you more than life itself! You are my everything, Mommy!

Heather had endured a rough twenty-four hours since they last communicated. She'd contracted a number of infections, which accounted for her mouth sores and a high fever; her body was covered in bruises – a symptom her doctor said was caused by the leukaemia that was now ravaging her body; as if that wasn't enough, she also had a large boil on her stomach that hurt like hell.

Not wishing to add to the stress Emma was already under in her enforced quarantine, she tried to keep this their latest chat bright and breezy. Just beneath the surface, however, she was beside herself with worry.

Given hospitals in Texas were affording priority to COVID-19 patients – exclusive priority in many cases – and the fact that Heather felt certain she'd die if she contracted the virus, she was trying holistic treatments for leukaemia. This she was prepared to share with her daughter. "I'm constantly juicing papaya," she said.

"I was going to suggest papaya, Mom," Emma said. She'd been researching cancer treatments online ever since she learned of her mother's condition.

"Yes it's a wonderful plant. I've discovered papaya leaf extract helps elevate tiny cells or platelets in the blood, and that's very important given leukemia causes platelets to drop to dangerous levels."

"That's great. But I heard papaya leaf extract doesn't taste very nice?"

"Ughh! Horrible," Heather agreed. "It's very bitter, but I'm adding lemon and honey to sweeten it and am actually developing a bit of a liking for it."

They then swapped notes on health supplements and other natural treatments they'd become familiar with in the course of the intensive research they'd both been conducting in recent days.

Heather revealed she was also using an infrared light therapy machine in addition to the various advanced natural supplements she was taking. Suppressing a yawn to conceal her tiredness, she closed her eyes for a moment.

"How are you feeling, mom?" a concerned Emma asked even though she already knew the answer to that.

"I'm feeling not too bad, darling," Heather lied, opening her eyes. "Some days better than others." While she did at times feel the treatments and supplements were making a positive difference, and that there existed some hope, she was feeling more tired every day and was finding it very difficult to breathe at times. And she was depressed, too. Depressed by her condition and by her deteriorating physical appearance, not to mention her continued separation from Emma at such a difficult time. Difficult for both of them.

On top of all that, she was experiencing a frightening visual anomaly no-one had warned her about. Not even her doctor or any of the other leukaemia patients with whom she was communicating online around the world. The bizarre and often eerie phenomenon made it seem as if nearby physical objects and landmarks were further away than they really were.

Heather first noticed the anomaly when reaching out for a pen on her desktop: the pen, and even her hand, seemed to be many feet away. Even now, as she looked at her dining table, which was only a few feet from the couch she currently occupied, it appeared to be some fifteen or twenty feet away.

Heather suspected she knew what caused the unnerving optical illusion, but she rarely allowed herself to dwell on it. She intuitively felt she was retracting further inside herself, and paradoxically away from planet Earth. Hence the physical world, and all objects in it, appeared much further away than they actually were.

Deep down, she had started thinking this was the beginning of the end.

Oh God, this must be what it feels like to die! We are sucked deeper and deeper inside ourselves and this physical world grows further and further away... Until finally it is no longer there...

"Mom, are you okay?" Heather asked. She'd noticed her mother seemed to be away somewhere.

"I need you to understand you must never give up on your dreams, sweetheart," Heather suddenly said without thinking and without acknowledging her daughter's question. It was her way of distracting herself and focusing on her beloved Emma instead. And it was something she had to say. She was pleased to see her daughter nodded, indicating she was on her wavelength.

Stifling another yawn, Heather continued, "Always keep trying... And understand that successful people are the biggest failures of all... They fail and fail until they finally succeed. Whereas others just give up at after a few failures, thinking that is their final fate."

Over the next few minutes, she shared with her daughter more of whatever wisdom she had gained throughout her life. Just in case she would not be around for her future. Her life stories – some happy, some sad – were all illuminating and often inspiring, and they included surprising admissions of her experiences as a teenager and young woman. Many of the intimate secrets shared were things Emma would never have guessed about her mom.

As she spoke, Heather thought about the importance of taking time to enjoy life and decided to tell her daughter a story. It was something Heather's grandmother had once told her. She said, "A wise man once was asked 'What amazes you the most in the universe?'. He answered, 'The human.' When asked why, he said, 'Because he sacrifices his health for accumulating money and then spends the money to protect his health, and he's so worried about his future he forgets to enjoy the present. So he lives as if he will never die, but then he dies as if he never lived'."

Tiring rapidly, Heather yawned and realized she could hardly keep her eyes open anymore. She gestured that she'd had enough and needed a break. "Now say it with me," Heather said. "You may be far from my eyes–"

"Mom, no. I don't want to!" Emma didn't want to hear let alone recite their usual farewell recitation. It was starting to sound, to her ears, more and more like a forever goodbye.

I hate all this space between us! The distance between me here in China and you in America… It feels like an epic chasm that can never be bridged.

Nearing the end of her tether, Emma looked away from the web-cam's lens. She thought about the innumerable situations and events that were preventing them from being together at that moment – the virus, the lockdowns and the red tape surrounding her replacement passport. Not forgetting the Chinese Communist Party blocking all Hubei province residents and visitors from leaving.

Not for the first time, she silently cursed the US Government for not finding a way to evacuate American citizens out of the region.

Heather persisted. "Say it with me… Please."

Emma reluctantly looked back at her mother.

In unison, mother and daughter said, "You may be far from my eyes, but you'll always be close to my heart."

20

..-. .- -.-. . ..--- ..-. .- -.-. .

SYDNEY, AUSTRALIA / JERUSALEM, ISRAEL

"I HONESTLY DON'T know what to do anymore."

Levi was only able to hear Esther not see her – for the time being at least.

While Esther was tucked up in her bed in Jerusalem, Levi was out walking in the sun again. He was determined to stay in shape and exercise during the ongoing Australian lockdown. But now that all the gyms in Sydney had been closed because of COVID-19 concerns, he had no choice but to get out into nature.

He had his phone in his pocket and was listening to Esther on his headphones. The restricted communication was because as he was walking across a narrow bridge at Parsley Bay Reserve and needed both hands free to maintain his balance. The family park, which was located in Vaucluse on Sydney's Eastern Suburbs, was popular due to its safe swimming area and children's playground.

As he walked over the bridge, Levi surveyed the beach below. He was heading for a bushland walking track, which would lead him to his destination – a waterfall.

"Somewhere along the way," Esther said, "I stopped believing there were any solutions. And I just started accepting it, looking to survive instead of thrive."

Levi reached the end of the bridge and took his phone out of his pocket so he could see Esther again. The pair had been talking for an hour, ever since Levi had left his home several miles away. Esther had opened up more about her lousy relationships with men in her past and the abuse she had suffered.

"Well," Levi said. "Maybe you have to find a way to believe again."

"Believe... in what exactly?"

Levi stepped onto the bush track and started following it. The waterfall was a place he had visited many times before. Usually when he had a lot on his mind or when he felt confused and had an important decision to make. He found being close to nature and listening to the sound of running water helped clarify things.

"Just believing in yourself and in life... Having faith to trust again. Not all men are assholes, you know?"

"I just fear I have nothing left... Only the capacity to feel pain."

"Maybe that's all you need," Levi replied. "To feel, I mean. And maybe feeling pain is a sign your heart is still open. It can eventually feel love again."

Esther nodded half-heartedly as if to say "possibly so". She then found herself yawning.

"Well it's late here," she said. "And I've got a headache."

"Can we talk again tomorrow, please?"

"Sure. Goodnight Levi. Have a nice bush walk".

"Thank you, Esther. Shabbat Shalom."

The screen faded to black as Esther turned her bedside lamp off. A split second later her webcam transmission switched off as well.

Levi reached the end of the bush track and arrived at the waterfall. The Parsley Bay Waterfall, to be precise.

Although just a small trickle of a waterfall that was only about twenty feet high, it had a tranquil, aesthetically-pleasing quality that Levi appreciated. The cliff-face behind it was what Australian nature enthusiasts refer to as a multi-step pyramid because of the different levels or tiers of rock formations. These essentially created a series of miniature waterfalls, and the effect was beautiful as well as calming.

Levi also knew that the waterfall and entire park area had been named after an early nineteenth century hermit called Parsley. He had apparently lived in a cave not far from it.

He was not here to consider the long-forgotten past however. Levi had a major decision to make in the present.

Just as he had reached out to Esther to say he'd begun thinking romantically of her again, an old flame of his had contacted him out of the blue.

Ayanda was that old flame and Levi had hardly been able to think straight since she had gotten in touch. It was quite an abrupt change given he had had a single-mindedness toward Esther for weeks. Now Ayanda had disturbed that.

He had to figure out if that was an unwelcome intrusion or not.

The other complication was he knew Esther was fragile and suffering from depression and PTSD. Furthermore, she had mentioned she'd been suicidal in the past, primarily due to the mental anguish and even self-hatred she'd experienced after being hurt by cruel men.

The last thing Levi wanted to do was to inadvertently become another cruel man in Esther's life. After all, he was aware he was gradually breaking down her defenses, and beginning to get close to her heart. By implication at least, he had been promising a lot romantically and realized he now needed to be completely sure he was as serious about her as he initially thought he was.

The stakes were high with Esther as given her mental health history he was aware he might actually be holding a woman's life in his hands. He didn't think she could survive yet another man destroying her trust.

His thoughts switched to Ayanda as he stood up on the rock formations and placed his hand under the waterfall.

Unfortunately, the tranquility of nature was unable to deliver him any clarity of mind on this occasion.

Levi's mind remained chaotic.

He knew that he needed to sort the mess out immediately and decide which woman his heart actually wanted to pursue.

21

..-. .- -.-. . ..--- ..-. .- -.-. .

BALI, INDONESIA / LONDON, UK

"ID MUM EVER tell you why she selected your name?"

Elijah shook his head. Seated on a bar stool in the house he was renting in Kuta, Bali, listening to his brother, he rocked back and forth on the stool slightly as he observed Mark who was once again in his home office in London.

There appeared to be something more relaxed looking about Mark on this day. Elijah did not know what it was, but the usual scowl he'd encountered on previous video chats was no longer there.

Mark suddenly held up an old, faded, black and white photo of their mother holding Elijah as an infant. "I recall her saying she had feelings about you when you were in the womb." It was a photo he'd found recently while doing some spring cleaning in his South Kensington apartment.

Elijah immediately felt emotional when he looked at their deceased mother holding him as a baby boy. He didn't look much older than a few months in the faded photograph, yet he appeared to be very alert.

"She felt like you were communicating with her while she carried you as a yet to be born baby," Mark said, "instilling her with wisdom and peace, she said… And even though she wasn't religious, she read somewhere while pregnant that Elijah was the only prophet in the Bible who reached heaven while still alive."

Mark abruptly grew more serious as he stared at Elijah on his computer screen.

"But now I wonder… what happened to you?"

Elijah nodded. He knew exactly what Mark was getting at. The truth stung him a bit, but it was a fair question in a way. After all, he had once been something of an overachiever growing up. He was a model student, he excelled at sports, and Mark although older often struggled to keep up. In many ways Elijah had been everyone's favorite.

"I fell from grace," Elijah eventually replied. "But I discovered out there on the road on my travels, we are all angelic beings that have been fallen for so long."

Mark shook his head and laughed a little. For once it wasn't really sarcastic or condescending, however. It was more just an acknowledgement that Elijah was so very different to himself.

What Elijah did not know, and the very reason they were having a slightly more conciliatory conversation, was that Mark had received some good news. The City of London financier he'd met with shortly before their last video call had changed his mind and agreed to invest in Mark's event management company. This had taken a little pressure off and given him the necessary space to sort out his myriad of family problems.

Elijah had also had some good news. His literary agent had just closed quite a substantial book deal with a major publishing house. There had actually been a bidding war between London publishers which had driven the price up.

Noticing Mark still looked reasonably chilled, Elijah took the opportunity to try again to describe what had happened to him on his travels. He recounted how a series of experiences, including the activation of his third eye, or pineal gland, had led to his awakening and greater self-awareness.

"My mind eventually expanded to the point where I could see the connections between all things. Where victim and perpetrator, enemy and friend, lover and foe, were revealed to be all the same thing. I saw God within every living thing, Mark."

Still not understanding any of it, Mark chuckled again. "All this stream of consciousness channeling shit you're doing...It sounds like you've lost your fucking mind!"

"Well," Elijah said, "maybe we need to lose our minds to be in our hearts again."

The brothers smiled at each other. Some common ground finally seemed to have been reached, even though neither knew how that had occurred exactly.

22

..-. .- -.-. . ..--- ..-. .- -.-. .

SYDNEY, AUSTRALIA / CAPE TOWN, SOUTH AFRICA

LEVI RESPECTFULLY BUT hastily pulled Ayanda's clothes off then ran his hands over her gorgeous, light-brown skin and luscious curves. He'd been desperate to grab her "hot, bangin' body", as he and some of his male colleagues called her hourglass figure, ever since he'd first started working with his African lover.

He'd just placed Ayanda on the king-sized bed of his downtown city hotel room overlooking Sydney's Hyde Park. Minutes earlier they'd finished walking hand in hand to the hotel from nearby Darling Harbour – after having worked a restaurant night shift together. A shift during which they'd flirted with each other almost non-stop.

Levi's mouth opened wide as his eyes roamed over her amazing body. She had a small waist, pert breasts, sexy thick thighs and a big, round ass.

Ayanda laughed with delight when she saw Levi's reaction upon seeing her naked form. Her eyes sparkled and she flashed her dazzling, white smile.

Levi found her entire personality fun, girlish and utterly thrilling.

Ayanda kissed him passionately.

"I wanted you inside me...all...night...long," she said.

Ayanda got up on all fours on the bed. She twerked her ass directly before him on the edge of the bed.

Needing no further encouragement, and feeling his throbbing hard-on needed action right that very second, Levi got onto the bed also. He grabbed her by the hips and prepared to enter Ayanda from behind, doggystyle.

Levi snapped out of his reverie as a dog barked somewhere in his neighborhood near his apartment in Vaucluse.

He had been reliving one of the best sexual experiences of his life. In fact, the more he remembered all the erotic details, the more he realized it'd actually been one of the best nights of his whole life. Period.

Levi's mind was still as foggy as it had been on his recent bush walk to the Parsley Bay Waterfall. Actually, he'd been unable to think clearly ever since Ayanda's email had arrived while he was on a video call to Esther.

Her email had been short and to the point:

> Hey, I was going through old emails trying to make sense of my life and there you were amongst it all. Are you still living in Australia and how are you handling this crazy lockdown? Hope everything is okay. Ayanda, XOXO

And yet, just that message alone had set off a million thoughts, emotions and sexual fantasies in Levi's head. It had also caused him much concern for he knew this complication undermined or even made a total mockery of everything he'd been promising Esther in relation to his intentions.

It also pissed Levi off that fantasizing about other women like this was a continuation of his past relationships. Sometimes those intense fantasies had led him to cheat on those he was in relationships with – or, in some cases, leave them for the other women he was lusting after.

Levi had assumed that was all just his younger, immature self who seemed determined to sow his wild oats as often as possible. He figured he'd grown out of desiring to fuck one woman after another.

You were wrong, dude!

"You know," Ayanda said, "I often wished I'd stayed in Australia a little longer."

Levi was now on a video chat with Ayanda. The purpose was to try to figure out if she might be the woman for him to pursue once the COVID-19 lockdown came to an end.

He looked at her smiling face, her caramel-colored skin and her shimmering hazel eyes. About ten year's younger than him, Ayanda was a twenty-something South African of predominantly Zulu ethnicity mixed with some Indian blood.

She was seated in the lounge of her home in Cape Town and Levi could see some type of native African artwork on a wall behind her.

"Why?" Levi asked. "Did you want to see more of this country?"

"No," Ayanda said, a little shyly. "I just… sometimes wonder… If my visa had not run out, and I had been able to continue being a waitress with you at that restaurant we were working at in Darling Harbour… "

Ayanda was aware she was rambling a bit. She cleared her throat then tried to summarize what she was trying to say. "If I had not had to return back here so soon after we started dating… I find myself wondering at times if something deeper, something more than all the fantastic sex we had, might have also developed."

Levi was finding it hard not to say he had been thinking exactly the same.

At that moment, a text message came in on his phone. He cursed inwardly when he saw it was from Esther. Levi had been trying not to think of her during this video call with Ayanda.

He quickly read Esther's text:

> Shalom, Levi! When did you want us to talk again? Perhaps,
> my time tonight, if that suits you also? I am looking forward to
> it, as your calm demeanor is really helping balance out my
> moods! Lots of Love, Esther

After reading it, Levi slowly looked back up at Ayanda on his laptop screen. She seemed to have changed position slightly, or else changed the angle of her webcam, as he could now see she was revealing a generous amount of cleavage.

23

..-. .- -.-. . ..--- ..-. .- -.-. .

WEST BANK, PALESTINE / RIO DE JANEIRO, BRAZIL

MARIAM AND HANAN were once again in conversation – a chat Mariam had initiated this time. As much as she hated to admit it, Hanan was the only person in the world she knew that she could talk to in the way she desperately needed to converse.

All the other people Mariam knew were on the West Bank or else in other occupied Palestinian territories such as the Gaza Strip, and therefore suffering just like she was. The pain of being refugees, and worthless ones at that, in their occupied lands was so relentless that everyone was just numb. Nobody truly believed in the possibility of a "Free Palestine" anymore. Nobody even dreamed of freedom or dared to discuss life improving.

Mariam's people had long since realized that hope was a dangerous emotion as it could easily lead to unrealistically high expectations. Given Palestinians had one of the highest suicide rates in the world, and the likes of the United Nations and Amnesty International had categorically termed much of the Palestinian territories as "unlivable" by any standard, there was no sense in considering or hoping for any positive future scenarios anymore.

Regardless, Mariam still found herself from time to time wanting to hope things would change. That some kind of miracle would occur against all odds. More so for her son than for herself.

"I'm just not functioning anymore," Mariam suddenly admitted.

Hanan, who was in her bedroom in Rio, felt deeply sympathetic toward Mariam. She had no idea why Mariam was suddenly opening up to her like this, but sensed something must have happened to her in Aida.

"Damn this year!" Mariam said. She was almost crying now. "2020 is seriously making me lose the plot! I can't concentrate, I can't sleep, I have been diagnosed as infected with this Godforsaken virus… And now I have to isolate myself from my own family… And on top of all that, the government is not providing us with any financial assistance at all… So now, being infected, I missed out on the UN job I interviewed for!"

The floodgates were really opening now and although Hanan felt sad for Mariam, she was also glad her fellow Palestinian was being honest about her depressing situation.

"But it's the little things that are making me go insane," Mariam said. "Like how my boy, Fadi, wants to be a professional tennis player… He's very good and visiting tennis scouts have said he has great potential. Maybe he could even be given a tennis scholarship in America or somewhere one day and get out of this hellhole prison we call home… But now I cannot afford his tennis lessons anymore!" Mariam finally burst into tears. "I don't know how I'm going to tell Fadi he will have to give up on his dream!"

Hanan jumped in, reminding Mariam she was now very wealthy and still wanted to give her money. "To help to take the pressure off, Mariam," she added

Mariam resisted again, but Hanan played on Mariam's fears about her son Fadi. Being a single mother in the West Bank, Hanan pointed out, was difficult enough without such financial woes and a pandemic being heaped on top of that.

Hanan glanced out her bedroom window as something moving outside attracted her attention. She saw it was the flapping wings of a large, bright, blue butterfly. It perched on the windowsill. She looked at its blue wings, which were stationary for the moment. They looked almost reflective in Rio's sunshine.

Hanan turned back to Mariam and suddenly smiled. "It's amazing how many opportunities life gives us. The opportunities the Lord provides us with are all around us, we just need to look for them."

Mariam looked offended all of a sudden. "So you are saying I should be grateful that the Lord is giving me this opportunity? That I should be grateful for you and your money?"

"No, Mariam," Hanan quickly replied. "I am saying that you could be my salvation. My golden opportunity to help. And that despite all my faults, and all my sins of the past, I can still be of service. For you see, I've been feeling lost for a long while. I couldn't find my place in this world anymore. I felt worthless too. I've been searching for ways to be of service. And if you let me help you, it will be assisting both of us. And your boy too. So will you just let me give to you? For the love of Jesus Christ, Mariam, please accept my gift!"

To Hanan's surprise, she eventually seemed to get thru to Mariam who actually began to nod through her tears.

"I need you to accept the money as much as you need the money," Hanan said. "So… Will you please allow me to take the burden off you, Mariam? So you can look after yourself and give Fadi the life he deserves?"

Mariam nodded again. "Alright, Hanan. I will allow myself to accept your gift, for the benefit of my child."

Both women were, for different reasons, overcome with emotion. They shared a beautiful moment as they looked into each other's tearful eyes via their web-cams.

24

..-. .- -.-. . ..--- ..-. .- -.-. .

AUCKLAND, NEW ZEALAND / ZÜRICH, SWITZERLAND

B YRON LOOKED PERCEPTIVELY at Albert for a moment, thinking about all the African had revealed. It was near the end of the podcast and he tried to think of some way to allow his guest to wrap things up for the audience watching.

"So, after everything you've witnessed and participated in… All the corridors of power you have walked in… What is the solution for the world, then? How can we ever create more equality and a fairer distribution of all this hidden wealth you've confirmed exists?"

"Debunking the scarcity narrative," Albert replied. He now had his feet up on his desk in his Zürich home office, although neither Bryon nor his Undergrounders watching could see that. "Just as you wrote in your *Sydney Morning Herald* article, the world's secret invisible economy is worth quadrillions of dollars. Quadrillions that represent undocumented wealth for humanity.

"Remember, there is almost infinite wealth on this planet right now. There exists thousands of times more gold and diamonds than is commonly acknowledged. But the world's financial systems are being manipulated by the few, at the expense of the many. And this leads to untold suffering for the poor and working classes of our world."

Upon speaking about the world's poor, Albert found himself thinking of his roots and his African heritage. He knew he had disrespected his ancestors. He'd discovered how the global elitists he worked for drowned poor nations like his native Ghana in a sea of debt in order to systematically bankrupt those nations. This was done primarily via loans given by the elitist-controlled World Bank and the International Monetary Fund. Once bankrupted by crippling interest rates, these nations would then be forever indebted – and be forced to give away most of their mineral riches and other assets to foreign powers instead of investing in their own citizens.

Being part of this system, and all too often a facilitator of it, Albert also knew that terms like the 'Third World' and 'impoverished nations' were essentially misnomers as they implied limited resources existed in those places. Growing up in Ghana, he knew his nation alone was actually teeming with assets and was not organically poor.

Albert glanced at a world map on his wall. His eyes lingered on West Africa – Ghana in particular. He hadn't been back there for sixteen years. There was nothing much to draw him back, but still even if he never set foot in Ghana again, he knew his heart was African and that could never change.

Until my heart beats its final beat and my soul leaves this Earth, my heart will always follow the African rhythm!

"Okay, I understand," Bryon said, "but how can we, The People, implement change?"

"A multitude of things. We need to audit the major banks for starters. The US Federal Reserve and the European Central banks, plus the Swiss private banks... Plus all the offshore bank accounts, as the Panama Papers was just the tip of the iceberg... This will educate the common people when they realize there are not trillions but quadrillions of dollars in undocumented wealth that's being concealed from us. And that there are many individuals who are trillionaires even though the Forbes Rich Lists never report this."

Byron nodded to indicate to Albert and the live audience of Undergrounders watching that he understood and agreed.

Albert continued, "We also need to stop being satisfied with tiny investments in the public domain... A new school here, a new homeless shelter there, a new hospital... Screw all those little things! We must demand a world without economic injustice. For history will prove there was never any excuse for such miseries. If we demand without any compromise, if eight billion people unite and stand up to demand better lives, I assure you everything we have ever wanted in our world comes into being."

Byron was about to say something, but Albert raised a finger to indicate he wanted to add one more thing.

"There always was enough for everyone. Poverty is, after all, an artificial construct conjured up by the financial gods who created this whole wicked economic system… A system which conceals the true wealth on the planet."

"Alright," Byron said. He was keen to wrap up the show. It had been an emotional podcast for him given how he'd learned Albert had essentially been a puppet master in his own life. "Do you have any final words for Undergrounders before we call it a day, Albert?"

"I sincerely hope that what I have said here can contribute to the growing awareness in the mass populace… That there is, contrary to what the Establishment tells us, enough wealth in the world to completely fix or at least help generate solutions for the biggest challenges our planet is currently facing."

25

..-. .- -.-. . ..--- ..-. .- -.-. .

LONDON, UK / BALI, INDONESIA

T HE BROTHERS WERE both more comfortable talking to each other now.

These video chats had been the most they had kept in touch for about a dozen years and they were surprised how much common ground they had discovered existed between them.

Elijah was in the middle of reminiscing about their childhood, which always seemed to make Mark less combative. Mark thought that was probably because almost all his memories of his younger brother as a boy were positive and heart-warming. He looked at Elijah on his phone as he listened.

Mark was in his car. He had just parked in an automatic carwash drive-thru machine in the West London suburb of Chelsea.

In Bali, Elijah stood outside in the backyard of the property he was renting. He smiled as he spoke to Levi. He then turned his camera to reveal a tree where the property bordered a cliff that overlooked the seaside town of Kuta. A treehouse could be seen perched on its lower branches.

"Remember when we used to play in our treehouse in Norfolk, Mark?"

Mark nodded as the automatic carwash began to do its job on his vehicle.

Elijah suddenly thought of something else from their childhood home in Norfolk, England. As he climbed the tree up toward the treehouse, he began to describe a memory. It was his earliest memory, he said.

To the best of his recollection, he and Mark were running around their back yard with wheelbarrows. There were coins in the barrows. And then Elijah accidentally tipped his wheelbarrow over and lost all his coins when they disappeared down a drain.

"All my pocket money allowance was gone," Elijah said. As he sat down inside the tree house there in Bali, he described how he cried as a little boy. "Those coins, the pocket money dad had given us, were all I had... So to my child's mind I felt like I had suddenly lost everything!"

Sitting in the carwash, Mark vividly remembered that day. Especially how he'd felt sorry for his little brother and decided to give him all his coins.

"I not only recall it, Elijah, but I remember I gave you every penny I owned and without even thinking."

What was mine was always yours. And vice versa.

The brothers smiled at each other as feelings associated with that childhood memory sprung forth. Suddenly they looked at each other and realized their family roots and brotherly connection were now overriding their recent differences.

"I love you, Mark. I'm sorry I wasn't there during important family times. And I'm asking for forgiveness."

Mark's steely exterior finally softened. He too was growing emotional.

"It was never about forgiving you, Elijah. It was just only ever about one thing... You coming home, being part of the family again. Or what's left of it."

Elijah felt like a massive weight had been taken off his shoulders.

"I have to go, sorry," Mark suddenly said. "Something's come up."

Elijah nodded and switched off the video feed. He climbed down from the tree house.

When he reached the ground, he felt like a different person. His brother's act of forgiveness had somehow restored him and his body literally felt lighter all of a sudden.

In London, nothing had come up at Mark's end. It was simply that he had become emotional and didn't want Elijah to see him like that. After driving out of the carwash, he parked his vehicle in the nearest parking space and shed a tear or two as he felt the strength of his bond with his baby brother. He was surprised as he couldn't actually remember the last time he'd cried or had even felt like crying.

Mark was also surprised how much he truly loved his only brother. For years, he'd convinced himself he despised Elijah and even told others that he didn't care for him. But now he realized he'd been lying to himself. Deep down their extremely close relationship – a relationship established since childhood – had not been severed. In a strange way, it actually felt more unbreakable than it ever had before.

26

..-. .- -.-. . ..--- ..-. .- -.-. .

WUHAN, CHINA / HOUSTON, USA

AS SHE TALKED to her mother again, Emma sat by the window of her Wuhan aparthotel room. "I never realized how much I love my country," she said, "until now when I can no longer get back there."

The young American glanced out her window at the bleak city of Wuhan. To her eyes, it looked like a ghost town. "I don't care about anything else, anymore."

Ain't that the truth!

She realized she did not care about what was occurring politically, what the death toll was for the COVID-19 pandemic, or even all the evil conspiracies she still believed were being carried out in the name of the virus.

"I just want to be home, back in America. And most of all, I want to be in your arms again, Mom!"

Emma remained depressed, even though she'd had two small pieces of good news in recent days.

One was that the U.S. Embassy in Beijing had finally contacted her. They had not only fast-tracked a replacement passport for her, but said they hoped within a week to be able to rescue Emma and all other American citizens in Wuhan.

The embassy official who had contacted her advised that because of her youth, and the fact she was a female and all alone, she was likely to be airlifted out of Wuhan in the first batch of returnees. And after that, she would be flown directly back to Houston.

She just prayed her mother would survive until then.

The other bit of good news was that Heather's leukaemia symptoms had lessened over the last forty eight hours or so. Her mother had reported that the mouth sores had mostly healed up and the bruises and boils were subsiding as well.

Emma didn't know whether or not it was the natural remedies that were helping, but regardless she hoped it would continue.

In Houston, Heather was relieved to be going through a less painful period. Internally it seemed as if her body was somehow healing itself. She just prayed she was not building up false hope in herself or in her daughter.

Deep down, mother and daughter still knew time could be running out. It made them treat each other extremely respectfully.

Emma felt she had matured so much since her mother's diagnosis. She now understood only love mattered. All the so-called important things she focused on previously were now a distant memory.

Thinking back on recent times before leaving America, Emma suddenly apologized for being rude to her mother during her late teens in particular. She added it was only because she felt like a confused teenager.

Heather instantly dismissed the apology.

"While raising you," Heather said, "I always felt you were the best daughter a mother could ever wish for. And you were the best thing that ever happened to me, Em."

After another hour of talking, Heather prepared to say goodbye for the day.

"Remember, you may be far from eyes... "

"Mom," Emma whispered, "please don't say it again."

"But you'll always be close to my heart," Heather said, completing the family ritual.

27

..-. .- -.-. . ..--- ..-. .- -.-. .

JERUSALEM, ISRAEL / SYDNEY, AUSTRALIA

ESTHER HAD BEEN thinking a lot lately. Or *contemplating*, as she liked to call it.

She'd come to the conclusion that the first thirty-eight years of her life could not have gone much worse even if she'd purposefully tried to screw things up.

What was likely to be about the first half of her life had mostly been a disaster. Not only being a teenage victim of Palestinian terrorism; not only clashing with much of the ideological thinking in the country she was born in; not only because she had been abused and humiliated by several male lovers – but also and especially because she had fully expected to have become a wife and mother by this point. In fact, she had wanted to experience that more than anything if she was being honest with herself.

The Israeli had been feeling a little more hopeful of late, however. She wanted to try to ensure the second half of her life would be better. And as she mentally reflected on all her memories and everyone she had ever known, she realized Levi was the only one who had truly reached her heart. She no longer found his persistence annoying. In fact, it endeared him to her and she was much more at ease chatting with him these days. He even made her smile sometimes.

Esther also reflected on his name and found it might hold some significance for her. Levi meant "attached" or "joined" in Hebrew, and she now felt attached or joined to him. She also knew that the root word of Levi was Levente, meaning a "knight" and she was coming round to the idea he really could become her knight in shining armor.

Levi was on her phone's screen at that very moment. He was walking home after having completed some hill sprints, which were part of his exercise routine, in Sydney's Eastern Suburbs.

Esther, who was folding some laundry in her apartment in Jerusalem, studied Levi carefully as he subtly presented, or alluded to, possible futures. She looked at his handsome, open face and all she felt was pure honesty from him. Her heart began to pulse or vibrate as she realized he was the one for her.

"I was planning to visit Israel later this year anyway," Levi said. "So if travel is allowed by then, can I take you out?"

"Yeah, sure."

"No pressure, of course. We can just meet as old friends, and see where it takes us. If there's a spark between us, then great. But from my end, I know there is chemistry between us already. It never died."

"So tell me, if by chance something happens between us again, and sparks fly... What might this life look like for us?"

Over the next few minutes of their video call, Levi painted a grand image of a future life for the pair of them. He talked about starting a family with Esther, the sort of lifestyle they might have, as well as the house he pictured them living in. He even mentioned the idea of having a big garden and growing their own vegetables.

Levi also indicated they could live in either Israel or Australia, it didn't bother him. He said he could start a restaurant in either country and therefore Esther could decide where they lived.

"Wherever you would be happiest, Esther."

Levi could see he was saying all the right things and had succeeded in finally melting her formerly icy heart.

Esther suddenly grew serious. "Levi... As you now know, I have been hurt so much in the past... And even you cheated on me before, and I just couldn't survive if you–"

"But I was just a kid then and you–"

"I know, but cheaters usually continue cheating. And more importantly, I've been through hell, wanted to kill myself, been on meds and sometimes I still hate myself... Mostly because of the shit men have done to me, plus that Palestinian terrorism incident I endured… So if there is any chance you are not completely serious about everything you're proposing, then I need you to leave me alone."

"I assure you... If I could have a date with any woman in the world right now, it would be you. And that's not because of sex, or not just that, but also because you're the only lady I am interested in exploring a life partnership with."

Ayanda suddenly flashed through his mind and he was momentarily overcome with guilt as he remembered the insane experiences he'd secretly shared with her over these last few days.

What the hell are you doing with your life, man?

He had been communicating with her more than he had with Esther and was in no doubt he'd become obsessed with his former African lover all over again. This knowledge only served to make him feel even more guilty.

PART THREE

TOGETHER APART

"Row, row, row your boat
Gently down the stream
Merrily, merrily, merrily, merrily
Life is but a dream."

–Anonymous
| *Row, Row, Row Your Boat*

28

- --- --. . - .... . .-. .- .--. .- .-. -

AUCKLAND, NEW ZEALAND

WAITEMATĀ HARBOUR BY night looked different to how Byron remembered seeing it on television or in video footage online. He could recall viewing specific helicopter or drone shots of Auckland from the air in the past, but the city on this evening revealed itself to have many more trees and rural spaces than he had been previously aware of.

To his left he could see the city's Sky Tower of the downtown and central business district area, and to his right were the lights of his own neighborhood in Devonport.

Beyond the naval suburb of Devonport, the distant glow of Takapuna and the rest of Auckland's North Shore was visible. East of that area was shrouded in darkness, but Byron knew that was where Rangitoto Island and Waiheke Island were located out to sea.

He was floating in the air almost directly above Auckland Harbour Bridge. He enjoyed the full three hundred and sixty degree view of Waitematā Harbour as he hovered high above like a bird lazily circling in the swirl of air currents.

Only fifteen minutes earlier he'd been tucked up in bed in his Devonport apartment. Now, as he was fully aware, he was having another out-of-body experience, or OOBE.

These mystical experiences had become so common that he was now fully accustomed to them. Astral traveling now seemed almost as natural to him as normal, waking life. And, to his great surprise, sometimes he found himself thinking that the immense freedom he felt while "out of the body" was perhaps the real normal and regular life was actually abnormal.

Byron was without warning projected out of the harbor location, out of New Zealand and beyond Earth itself. He found himself elsewhere in the universe, floating freely in Outer Space. He had no idea where exactly, but this was another thing that often occurred during his OOBE's – rapid teleportations to distant locations, whether they be elsewhere on Earth or somewhere else in the universe.

Using his mind or willpower to direct his movements – something he'd learnt to do while astral traveling – he turned around in the vastness of space and suddenly discovered the rings of Saturn were directly ahead of him. Before he knew it, he was floating through the countless small particles of the ring system that orbits the planet. They felt cool and icy on his face as his astral body drifted through each layer of the rings, carried along by invisible and irresistible space currents.

Byron looked at the massive planet of Saturn looming up ahead. It reminded him of effervescent drinks as he could see fizzy-like storms of energy exploding all over the planet's pale yellow, gaseous surface.

He suddenly noticed a large rock orbiting Saturn in the rings and traveling at speed.

Holy shit! Is that a meteor fragment?

He felt his heart rate spike as he realized the rock was coming straight at him. And it was too late to avoid being hit by it.

Byron sat bolt upright in his bed. He'd been jolted back to his Devonport apartment's bedroom and was once more in regular, waking consciousness. This was also something that happened with OOBE's he'd discovered: whenever he feared anything, he would instantly return to his physical body, totally alert.

He didn't know why he had just visited Saturn in his latest OOBE. The only thing he knew about astrology was that he seemed to recall the Ancients believed the planets – especially Jupiter, Saturn, Mars and Venus – had a major influence over the Earth and human affairs.

Remaining awake in bed for a while to gather his thoughts, Byron realized he was now at almost total peace with his nightly supernatural experiences. In fact, he'd found himself wanting to explore the inner or astral realms, or other dimensions, or whatever it was he was experiencing, more and more.

And although he'd initially thought the OOBE's were a big distraction, he now felt differently. That change in opinion was because he felt they had made him look at his daily life in a completely different way. He now believed he could see a dream-like quality to life in general.

The more he experimented with the concept of his daily world and career and relationships all existing within in a dream, the more his life situation had improved. Things had picked up financially, and in his career, too, and he felt less fearful than before. Less fearful even about death because he believed OOBE's were a glimpse into what it would eventually be like once his physical body died and he left it and projected out in another form.

As his mind or consciousness had expanded of late, he now sensed his daily life was somehow being dreamed into being by him every step of the way. Additionally, he found that when he focused on being the projector of his own reality then things would turn out for the best. Whenever he experienced or observed the dreaminess of life then, straight away, everything always felt more fluid, more possible and less dense.

Byron had decided his goal in his life from now on was to be more playful and child-like and to treat life with some kind of positive irreverence.

As he stared up at his bedroom ceiling, he wondered how Albert was doing in Switzerland and whether he would survive. The Ghanaian's prediction that he would soon be killed for the information he'd leaked during the Underground Knowledge podcast preyed on his mind.

29

- --- --. . - .... . .-. .- .--. .- .-. -

WEST BANK, PALESTINE

ARIAM RUFFLED HER son's hair then laughed for the first time she could remember in many months. Or many years perhaps.

Thirteen year old Fadi was seated at the dining table of their new home. It was situated at one corner of Aida Refugee Camp – a quieter corner which had slightly more privacy than their previous apartment's location.

Mariam and Fadi had moved into the home after Hanan's monetary gift had arrived from Brazil. They'd relocated with Mariam's ailing, elderly parents and so it was a rare single-family apartment in Aida. Usually different refugee families lived together in communal homes, just as Mariam had in her last home.

Fadi was doing his homework. He was in his first year of high school and had just returned from school.

Now that Mariam no longer had to worry about earning survival money each week, she had set herself up as a full-time carer for her parents. She also could afford to be a stay-at-home mother and give Fadi all the attention he needed as he transitioned into puberty.

She looked down at a piece of paper he was writing on.

Fadi was learning Latin and his homework task was to translate some of the Latin into Arabic.

Anno MMXX was the last bit of Latin he needed to translate. Fadi thought carefully for a few seconds then, with his pencil, he wrote "Year 2020" in Arabic.

As Mariam stared at her boy, she felt happy he could continue on with his dream of becoming a professional tennis player. It wasn't important that he necessarily achieved his dream, she thought, because she knew he would need a lot of luck to become a pro. For her it was something much deeper than that. It stemmed from being a life-long refugee; it hadn't helped either that she had often been restricted in what she could strive for, or even dream of, in life.

Not everyone can achieve all their dreams. But everybody deserves the freedom to pursue their dreams.

Having now completed his homework, Fadi looked up at his mother.

Mariam saw in her son's eyes the one thing many people had tried to suppress and therefore effectively destroy in Palestinians:

Hope.

Those people included ultra-Zionist politicians and their Israeli soldiers, anti-Arab people in the international community, certain traitorous Palestinians, and even herself at times.

30

`- --- --. . - .... . .-. .- .--. .- .-. -`

LONDON, UK / BALI, INDONESIA

A RELAXED MARK and his wife Vicky sat close together as they drank coffee in the lounge of their South Kensington apartment. Tensions between them had eased significantly in recent weeks. In fact, they were maybe even beginning to fall in love with each other again. As a result, Vicky had decided not to abort and was preparing to give birth to their child.

Mark didn't know how their marriage had survived especially as it had felt doomed at the start of the year when all the chaos surrounding the Coronavirus pandemic had begun. But now that he was able to look back at the year to date with the wisdom that hindsight often brings, he could see that in a strange way being forced to slow down and stop working as much had helped Vicky and himself. Their lives had reverted to a simple existence and they were able to get to know each other at a deeper level, like never before.

Watching the couple drinking coffee at that very moment courtesy of yet another video link was Elijah. He was still in Bali, but was literally packing his bags and preparing to finally leave the Kuta property he had rented all year. His next destination: Bali's Ngurah Rai International Airport and then onto England.

Elijah had originally planned to leave Bali earlier, but the editor behind the major book publishing deal he'd signed asked him to do extensive rewrites. And so he had prolonged his stay, figuring the nature and tranquility of the South East Asian paradise was the perfect place to finish off the manuscript without being disturbed.

He also knew the sooner he completed the rewrites and met in full the terms of his writing contract, the sooner he'd receive the full balance of monies owed by his publisher. It was a substantial sum which would allow him to provide for more than himself once he returned to London to live.

The reason Mark and Vicky were having this video chat with him was to discuss his pending arrival at London Heathrow Airport. They were also keen to establish whether or not he would need to be quarantined for a period upon arrival due to COVID-19 safety concerns.

Britain's Prime Minister Boris Johnson had recently plunged the country into another nationwide lockdown in response to a reported second wave of the virus and laws were changing constantly. Only minutes before the video call, Mark had after a lot of effort gotten a clear answer from authorities on what protocols British citizens returning home would have to go through.

Elijah was about to ask more about the ramifications of a potential quarantine upon his arrival in the UK, when suddenly his six-year-old niece, Sophie, walked into the camera's frame.

Sophie sat on Vicky's lap and looked at Elijah's face on the screen of Mark's laptop on the coffee table before them.

Elijah had never met her, or even chatted with her via video before, but as soon as he saw her sweet, innocent face he felt himself melt inside. He instantly wanted to hold Sophie and protect her.

Blood really must be thicker than water!

Sophie turned to Mark. "Uncle Mark, who is that?"

"This is your other uncle... Elijah... He's coming home soon, to look after you."

"Hey, Sophie!" Elijah said enthusiastically. His loud voice boomed through the laptop's speakers.

Even though Mark had agreed some time ago to give Elijah a chance and allow him to adopt Sophie, he was very mindful of his brother's lengthy history of not delivering on promises. He did not want to get a six year old's hopes up only to have Elijah flake out and ghost on the poor girl. So, to be safe, he was only planning to introduce her to Elijah once his brother was finally back on English soil again.

But now that Sophie had spontaneously inserted herself into the video chat, there was nothing Mark could do to prevent the interaction. Besides, he really did believe Elijah had changed.

"I'm sorry for your loss, Sophie," Elijah said. "I know your mother, our sister, was a light that can never be replaced. But I promise you I am going to look after you. Forever and ever!"

"Thank you," a slightly confused Sophie eventually said.

Elijah saw Vicky whisper something into Sophie's ear.

Sophie leaned close to the camera. "See you soon, Uncle Elijah."

"Oh yes, I'll be with you soon!" Elijah smiled.

Sophie waved into the web-cam.

Standing alone in his Bali rental property, Elijah waved back at her.

31

- --- --. . - .... . .-. .- .--. .- .-. -

JERUSALEM, ISRAEL / SYDNEY, AUSTRALIA

"WELL," ESTHER SAID. "Until lockdown is over and international travel resumes, we can maybe try to practice love in isolation, right?"

Levi looked at Esther on his screen. Observing her inside her Jerusalem apartment, he could see he had somehow made a positive impact on her. Esther now looked so much more carefree than before. She was also smiling and looked more like the vivacious young woman he had fallen in love with almost two decades earlier.

Levi's mind wandered yet again to the crazy happenings that had occurred to him since Ayanda had gotten in touch with him out of the blue. His old desires for the South African beauty had completely consumed him and he even felt sure he was falling in love with her. They had not only been communicating multiple times a day, but had had webcam-sex together. And seeing Ayanda orgasm on camera as she pleasured herself only inches from her web-cam in Cape Town had driven Levi wild with lust. Especially as he'd not been able to be physically close to a woman during the entire Australian lockdown period.

Just as he had been visualizing in detail a possible future life with Esther, he began to start doing the same with Ayanda. And he was pretty damn sure it wasn't just sexual. He could also picture himself hanging out with her, marrying her, impregnating her, and various other things he hoped to do with whoever became his life partner. She was not just a sexual goddess, but also a very good person as well.

But then one night he'd woken up about three o'clock in the morning after dreaming his father had visited him. He sat there in bed in the dead of night thinking again about his deceased father. Levi cried, remembering how he'd been too young at the time to appreciate all the things his father had done for him. How his father had instilled in him a sense of self-worth that was so strong that nobody could ever take it away from him.

Levi also remembered what he'd once told Esther: that he'd realized, by his father's example, it was not about building the best house, but rather the best *home*. Any building, no matter how humble its structure, that had a strong family unit inside teeming with love and respect for all its family members, was always worth more than the greatest mansion on Earth, he'd told her.

It was at that moment, lying alone in bed in the middle of the night, he'd realized Esther had the strongest family values of any woman he'd ever known. She was all about pure respect and kindness, and he knew she would make a fantastic mother.

As much as he desired Ayanda and cared for her, he'd realized right then that Esther was the woman he wished to spend the rest of his life with.

Esther's the one for me... and Israel is where my heart lies!

Levi's mind snapped back to the present and he looked at Esther on his phone's screen.

"Yeah, sure," Levi finally said in response to Esther's suggestion they could practice love in isolation. "Let's do that."

Esther smiled again. It was a smile that melted Levi's heart.

32

- --- --. . - .... . .-. .- .--. .- .-. -

AUCKLAND, NEW ZEALAND / ZÜRICH, SWITZERLAND

"**I HAVE BEEN** contacted by so many people since your confession a few weeks ago," Byron said. The Kiwi was in the middle of another podcast, a follow-up episode, with Albert. He was seated outside in a park on Auckland's North Shore while Albert was once again in his home office in Zürich.

The last podcast had gone viral online and people all over the planet had started demanding answers. Answers from elected officials and certain influential people Albert had exposed. Byron had also been contacted by various media outlets and it seemed likely he would once again have some kind of journalistic career as an indie journo or even as an investigative reporter for a major news media organization.

"Albert, I have to tell you the public response and global interest has been phenomenal," Byron enthused. "So can you provide an update to Undergrounders of your present situation? And are you getting any blowback after the recent publicity?"

"I've received word from my elite sources in the higher-ups," Albert said. "And it seems I will be silenced, one way or another. Before I leak more explosive secrets. My days are probably numbered. There is too much money and too much power at stake."

Byron wasn't surprised. "I'm very sorry to hear that, Albert."

"Don't be. The thing is... I don't feel sad. This was the highly predictable result of my actions. And also... When I look in your eyes, Byron, I see... "

Albert paused as he looked at Byron's face on his screen.

"This may be hard for you and your viewers to understand given you and I have never met in person. But I never had a family of my own... So when I consider the wrongs I did to you and how you forgave me... And also the way we've kept in touch and become friends over the last few weeks... Even after the wrongs I did to you... Well, I realize that... "

An emotional Albert hesitated. Byron patiently waited for him, taking care not to interrupt his guest's thought processes.

"You're like the son I never had," Albert said at length.

Byron couldn't hide his surprise. He felt sorry for Albert for he knew if he was the closest he had to a son then this probably meant he was a very lonely individual.

Albert continued, "The hardest thing to get in this world is substance. It cannot be given to you, it cannot be inherited genetically either. It must be earnt. You have that, Byron. Real substance. And nobody can ever take it away from you... So, *please*, go ahead and become the type of uncompromising investigative journalist you aspired to be."

As the New Zealander registered Albert's sincerity, he marveled at the remarkable turn of events. That this man who had once taken so much from him had now given him a new chance at life. But more than that, he now understood Albert's life had been complicated and he was not an example of good or evil. Rather, he figured the Ghanaian, like most people, was duality personified and a mixture of both good and bad.

33

HOUSTON, USA / WUHAN, CHINA

"**W**HERE THE WAVE of moonlight glosses," Heather said. "The dim gray sands with light, Far off by furthest Rosses, We foot it all the night, Weaving olden dances, Mingling hands and mingling glances, Till the moon has taken flight."

Heather was reciting poetry into her phone for her daughter on the other end of their latest video connection.

Emma was still in Wuhan. However, US officials in China had guaranteed she would be rescued within twenty-four hours along with various other Americans. From there, she had been promised she would be back in Houston within days.

However, looking at her mother, Emma was not completely certain she would still be alive by then. She looked exhausted. It seemed all the life had drained from her face. And she seemed so frail and fragile, almost skeletal to Emma's eyes.

Heather was sitting in a wheelchair in Houston's Cockrell Butterfly Center. The facility, which was essentially a large glasshouse rainforest habitat complete with a manmade lake and waterfall, was an extension of the city's Museum Of Natural Science. The center was officially closed and off limits to the public, as was the museum itself, because of COVID-19 restrictions.

Fortunately, Heather knew one of the caretakers and, given her dire medical circumstances, she had been allowed to visit alone. She normally visited the facility every year and had wanted to revisit at least one more time – whilst she was still able to.

The caretaker was an overprotective girlfriend who had known her since high school. She'd insisted Heather be put in a wheelchair and guided around to make sure she did not have a mishap.

Heather was enjoying a private moment with her daughter via modern technology as the considerate caretaker sat on the far side of the glasshouse-enclosed rainforest. Surrounded by various species of butterflies, of all shapes, sizes and colors, Heather continued reciting the poem…

> *"To and fro we leap*
> *And chase the frothy bubbles,*
> *While the world is full of troubles*
> *And anxious in its sleep."*

Emma knew her mother was reciting the Nineteenth century poem *The Stolen Child* by W. B. Yeats.

It was Heather's favorite poem and something her Irish grandmother had recited to her shortly before her death when Heather had been a teenager just like Emma was now.

Heather continued…

> *"Come away, O human child!*
> *To the waters and the wild*
> *With a faery, hand in hand,*
> *For the world's more full of weeping*
> *than you can understand."*

Emma could barely look at her dying mother. She understood this may be her mom's way of saying goodbye, but she did not want to face that reality.

Even though she noticed her daughter look away, Heather remained strong and continued regardless…

> *"Where the wandering water gushes*
> *From the hills above Glen-Car,*
> *In pools among the rushes*
> *That scarce could bathe a star,*
> *We seek for slumbering trout*
> *And whispering in their ears*
> *Give them unquiet dreams;*
> *Leaning softly out*
> *From ferns that drop their tears*
> *Over the young streams."*

Very familiar with the poem, Emma began to mouth the words silently as her mother continued the recital…

> *"Come away, O human child!*
> *To the waters and the wild*
> *With a faery, hand in hand,*
> *For the world's more full of weeping*
> *than you can understand."*

Heather suddenly lapsed into a coughing fit. It was a heavy, wheezing sound. So weak was she now, she was unable to continue her recital. Alarmed by the sudden coughing, her caretaker friend hurried to check on her, but Heather gestured she was fine, sending her back to where she'd been patiently sitting.

Emma bravely decided to continue reciting the poem on behalf of her mother…

"Away with us he's going,
The solemn-eyed:
He'll hear no more the lowing
Of the calves on the warm hillside
Or the kettle on the hob
Sing peace into his breast,
Or see the brown mice bob
Round and round the oatmeal chest."

Heather looked up as a large, blue butterfly landed on her lap. She studied it, enchanted, as it lingered for a moment, fluttering around on her lap before heading toward the manmade lake where it hovered for several heartbeats as if to admire its beautiful reflection in the lake's glassy surface.

Having now recovered slightly, Heather joined in again. Mother and daughter recited the last stanza of Yeats' poem, together, in unison…

"For he comes, the human child,
To the waters and the wild
With a faery, hand in hand,
For the world's more full of weeping
than he can understand."

34

- --- --. . - .... . .-. .- .--. .- .-. -

BALI, INDONESIA

ELIJAH COULD SMELL the tropical flowers as he breathed deeply during a meditation on Kuta Beach.

With his eyes closed, he could hear the waves crashing into the shoreline as he sat there in the lotus position. Each breaking wave was in perfect unison with his breathing cycle. He took that as a sign from the universe that everything was now spiritually aligned, or it soon would be.

Synchronicity, baby!

Elijah was scheduled to depart Bali for London in the next few hours. He'd come to the beach to get in one last meditation session. It was partly to satisfy himself and partly to satisfy the hardcore group of global followers he had attracted of late. They liked to regularly participate in the online group meditations he freely offered to genuine spiritual seekers.

The virtual observers were remotely viewing Elijah's morning meditation via his phone, which he'd placed on a rock before him.

"Man," he suddenly said, eyes still closed. "How did we get here?"

Elijah took another deep breath, before he opened his eyes and looked directly into his phone's camera. He adjusted the phone's position on the rock in order to frame himself slightly better.

"And what the hell is this year all about?"

Elijah shook his head and smiled before closing his eyes once more as if to intuitively seek answers.

After a few more deep inhalations and exhalations, he addressed those he was communicating with once more.

"Can there be a silver lining to all this madness?"

Oblivious to the sounds of a few locals on the beach nearby, he thought deeply about the year to date. Various things jumped out from within his memories and appeared in his mind's eye as short, sharp mental flashbacks. They included the spread of the virus, the lockdowns, mask wearing, conspiracy rumors of coming mandatory vaccines, protests and anarchy surrounding Black Lives Matter, the highly controversial Trump versus Biden US Presidential election and the myriad of other social upheavals.

He also thought about how COVID-19 seemed to have polarized the public. Specifically, all the philosophical debates still raging on about society's need to protect *the masses* versus the need to uphold the rights and freedoms of *the individual*.

The world's secret invisible economy sprang to mind. An economy apparently worth quadrillions. The same invisible economy Albert, his Ghanaian follower, had professed to having intimate knowledge of in a recent podcast.

He went deeper into his mind's eye and waited for some intuition.

"But, what if… What if there's been something orderly going on this year? What if it seems like random chaos because our ant-like human brains simply cannot even begin to conceive of an organized structure behind all these wild events? What if something unfolds, in time, to show us everything was in perfect, divine order?"

Elijah briefly looked at his audience on his phone's screen. He could see four of his followers were looking back at him at that very moment. He immediately recognized them as Hanan, Levi, Albert and Heather, and he recalled they respectively resided in Rio de Janeiro, Sydney, Zürich and Houston.

Each had subscribed to his video channel or spiritual travel blog in the last year or so and had been following his teachings. From there they had begun to interact with him personally and receive free guidance from him on problems or challenges they were facing in their own lives.

Looking into the eyes of his subscribers, he said, "Why don't you all share with the group what steps you have each taken to align with your soul's inner journey?"

35

- --- --. . - .... . .-. .- .--. .- .-. -

RIO DE JANEIRO, BRAZIL

H ANAN FELT AS if Elijah was addressing her personally as she studied him on her cell phone's screen. She was inside her car in the carpark outside a fast-food outlet. She'd parked there to avoid becoming gridlocked in Rio's notorious traffic.

The Palestinian had been visiting a client and she'd planned to be home in time for the video conference she was currently participating in. However, the heavy traffic had put paid to that plan.

Looking intently at the Bali-based video conference host, she said, "I have spent much of this year following many of your teachings and trialing your methods and meditation techniques, Elijah. And I am starting to feel better about myself. I even sleep easier at night. Whilst it's true I needed to do something good to atone for my sins, I also realized in the process that I needed to forgive myself... For deep down I now can see I was falling into self-hatred."

Hanan went on to reveal to Elijah and the group that earlier in the year she had faced her past and addressed what she called "her worst sin ever".

Over the months since she had finally gotten Mariam to accept her monetary gift, Hanan had been diligently working on the next phase of her personal project. It was to try to help Mariam, and her son Fadi, migrate to Brazil.

But it proved to be no easy task. In fact, that was an understatement.

Hanan thought back to a depressing discussion she'd had with Israa, an Egyptian-Brazilian immigration lawyer based in São Paulo. She had been referred to her as a trustworthy lawyer who specialized in helping Arabs migrate to Brazil.

Israa had informed her that under the latest legislation Palestinian refugees were rarely permitted to relocate to another country. She'd said, "Basically, a refugee living in any of the camps in the Occupied Palestinian Territories needs a lot of money, which no one has due to complete poverty there. *And* they would also need strong relationships with those in Israeli authority. So whilst it's technically not impossible, in reality one would need a series of miracles to occur to be able to relocate to a country like Brazil."

There were also problems with passports, Israa had added. Like many refugees living in Gaza or on the West Bank, Mariam did not have the necessary ID or official documentation required to procure a Palestinian Authority Passport.

In addition, only some countries accepted or acknowledged the Palestinian passport, and, because of biased media coverage and propaganda, many ordinary Palestinians were wrongly assumed to be terrorists. To add to these complications, there was no standardized passport for Palestinians. There were in fact seven different agencies issuing versions of passports and each agency claimed their version was the only official one.

And finally, Israa had informed Hanan of yet another potential stumbling block. Passport and migration laws along with other travel-related regulations changed after every conflict, which was every year or two on average. Therefore, a Palestinian refugee could go through all the red tape and finally be granted some kind of passport and visa to migrate to a foreign country, only to find everything was for nothing or their passport had been invalidated.

Although Hanan had managed to depart Palestine, it was during a less complicated era with less terrorism and, unlike Mariam, she wasn't a refugee.

She had been about to give up trying to help her friend when the son of the recently deceased Israeli owner of the architectural firm she worked for offered his assistance. He'd promised to pull some strings as he had direct connections to senior politicians in Israeli Prime Minister Benjamin Netanyahu's administration.

"The Lord suddenly illuminated the path forward for me," Hanan informed the group. "It was suddenly looking very likely that Mariam and her son would be able to migrate to Brazil. We still had more work to do, but I held that new reality in my mind... That Mariam and Fadi will be able to live free from violence and fear here in Brazil.

"And lo and behold, against all odds, it is about to crystallize... My team and I have only yesterday secured passports and other relevant documentation, as well as a Brazilian migration visa. This has all been approved by Israeli and Palestinian authorities!"

Byron clapped and the others on screen all looked happy for her as well.

Hanan smiled back at them. As she heard others in the group begin to clap in acknowledgement of her achieving the great assignment, she suddenly felt a wave of happiness as well as great relief.

A solitary tear slid down her face.

36

- --- --. . - .... . .-. .- .--. .- .-. -

ZÜRICH, SWITZERLAND

ALBERT WAS THE next one to speak on the video call with Elijah and his group of spiritual seekers.

Sitting outside a café on the shore of Lake Zürich, he told the group about his earlier podcast experience during which he'd divulged truths to Byron. Truths he considered an important part of his *redemption*.

Albert reiterated that he'd flagged to Byron he planned to leak more truths and start naming bigger names. He also revealed he'd received word his life was now in danger.

"But, I am comfortable with all this," he said. "I've come to believe what you've been saying in your videos, Elijah… That our souls are all on an epic journey through the universe and this lifetime here on Earth is just a brief stop-over in a much bigger travel itinerary. So I honestly feel what's most important is I have aligned myself to my soul's true nature… And if they kill me now, well, who cares? Not me, really!"

Albert chuckled at his own joke. He couldn't believe how lightly he was treating life and death now, but that inner irreverence was an honest reflection of how he felt about his situation. And that was thanks, in no small way, to the teachings Elijah had shared. He had also been practicing some ancient Indian meditation techniques Elijah had taught him, which always seemed to connect him to some energy force greater than himself.

"There's a poem," Albert said, "by the ancient Greek poet Aeschylus that I think summarizes why I lost my way in life... Why I had so much knowledge, but never any wisdom, until now." He paused as a waitress delivered his coffee order to his table. "Even in our sleep, pain which cannot forget falls drop by drop upon the heart until, in our own despair, against our will, comes wisdom through the awful grace of God."

Having finished reciting Aeschylus' poem, Albert began drinking his coffee. He then looked out at the lake. Something about the glistening water in the sunshine reminded him of Lake Bosumtwi in his native Ghana.

His mind drifted back to his childhood growing up in the small West African nation during the 1970's. He recalled long days of freedom playing on the shores of the ancient crater lake with other boys of his Ashanti tribe.

He also remembered what it was like to be that innocent child – long before he had sinned so frequently and before he had aided and abetted the greedy moguls who had recruited him in adulthood.

As he felt the purity of his boyhood self once more within his heart, Albert shed a solitary tear.

37

- --- --. . - .... . .-. .- .--. .- .-. -

SYDNEY, AUSTRALIA

LEVI WAS NEXT up in this video carousel of Elijah's little group of spiritual seekers.

He was sitting beside other passengers inside the noisy, crowded terminal of Sydney International Airport and was preparing to board a direct flight to Jerusalem.

Australia had only that day reversed its ruling that Australian citizens be prevented from traveling internationally. True to his promise to Esther, he was not wasting any time to go straight to Israel to further develop their relationship in person.

"This has been the most insane year, guys," Levi said. "But I have learnt a lot about myself and I've tried to grow and evolve and become a real man… Like my father was… If I can convince Esther to marry me, then it will be a bit of a case of that old saying… All's well that ends well!"

Levi paused as he handed over his passport to a check-in employee. The staffer checked his passport then handed it back.

"So wish me luck, guys! I am trying to win the heart of the lady I have realized was always the great love of my life."

Everyone else on the video call cheered, wolf-whistled or provided words of encouragement.

"But the thing is," Levi continued, "I can honestly say I am no longer coming from the selfish state I previously operated from. I'm no longer an immature prick and that's partly due to you pushing me to keep working on myself, Elijah."

Elijah smiled in acknowledgement and Levi nodded back to him.

The Australian continued, "You see, I genuinely want the best for Esther... and if by chance we meet and no romance develops then I will try to be a good friend to her instead. So I finally feel that I love someone more than I love myself. And that gives me confidence that I will always treat her as she deserves to be treated."

What Levi didn't mention was there was another reason he was happy with his decision: he was coming around to the idea that he would one day do what Jews termed "make Aliyah", meaning relocate to Israel.

His father had not only instilled a sense of self-worth and Jewish pride in him since he was young, he'd also taught him that Israel was crucial for the survival of the tiny, persecuted minority that Jews were.

Every inch of Levi's being believed Israel's existence was a legitimate and divine part of the tumultuous, centuries-long story of Judaism in a world full of anti-Semites, and he'd finally matured to a point where he was ready to be of service to Israel.

I want to be a good Israeli citizen alongside my brothers and sisters in my Jewish homeland. More than that...I have to be a good Israeli citizen.

Levi was aware that being surrounded by Arab nations – nations whose citizens, in the main, wanted to destroy all traces of Zionism in the Middle East – virtually guaranteed Israelis faced a future of tumultuous chaos. A future of continuing wars and terrorism not to mention criticism from what he viewed as a misinformed international community.

Regardless, he had finally reached the point where he was willing to personally contribute to Israel's future wellbeing no matter the sacrifice.

Whatever it takes. Even though that means sacrificing the life I've carved out for myself here in peaceful Australia, the Lucky Country, and facing a future of uncertainty in my spiritual homeland Israel.

He smiled to himself. Having Esther as his wife, or as a good friend at least, would confirm he'd made the right decision.

38

HOUSTON, USA

THE LAST ONE in Elijah's group to speak was Heather. She was on the balcony of her apartment in downtown Houston. The American revealed she'd implemented many of the meditation and breathing practices Elijah had taught her. And that she had made peace with her life and had all but lost her fear of death.

The surprising thing was Heather was actually doing well. She was a lot stronger than before and her prognosis was good.

Since the lockdown in Houston had ended, she had been able to get treatment within the medical system. "Emma, my daughter, convinced me to get treatment within mainstream medicine for my leukaemia. But the good news is I found a doctor who utilizes both mainstream medicine and complimentary or natural medicine."

Heather didn't mention she had received chemotherapy as well as a stem-cell transplant and the results had been much better than expected. The doctors had even used the word "miraculous" to describe her rapid turnaround.

"So, after preparing to die, and being at peace with that and surrendering to the universe, it now appears the universe has other plans for me. Who knows, I may even live to be an old lady!"

Everyone on the video call, including Elijah, clapped and cheered.

"But what really pleases me even more than my own survival," Heather said, "is that" – she paused to look inside her apartment from the balcony where she saw her beloved Emma sitting on a couch and reading something on her phone – "my daughter is back home safe with me."

Heather smiled at her daughter who looked up at that very moment as if sensing she was being talked about.

Emma had been successfully rescued by US officials and flown out of Wuhan to Beijing. From there she'd been flown in a government-chartered plane direct to Houston where she'd enjoyed an emotional reunion with her mother.

The young American was engrossed in the Kindle ebook version of a new release book she'd purchased earlier. It was an acclaimed poetry and prose publication titled *The Gulag Village Green* by British author Harry Whitewolf. As she read, Emma felt like she'd found a kindred spirit in this new author she'd discovered. Whitewolf's irate yet insightful writing was highlighting to her many of the current issues in society she was most concerned about. In particular, the loss of freedoms that had occurred around the world during the year.

Emma had witnessed firsthand all the COVID-19 regulations as they were progressively rolled out in China, and she'd observed the same level of draconian laws being imposed on citizens globally as the virus spread beyond China's borders.

While reading, Emma had an anti-lockdown song playing in her earphones. She had it repeating on loop and was singing along with it every so often. Titled *Little Seed Big Tree*, it was by British alternative rock singer Ian Brown and it had recently gone viral. The track had a similar rebellious, angry spirit to Whitewolf's book, and the lyrics included controversial terms and phrases like "Masonic lockdown", "new world order", "forced vaccine", "mass mind manipulation", putting "your muzzle on", and planting a "microchip" inside "every woman, child and man".

The end of year was fast approaching, and yet Emma had noticed much of the COVID legislation remained in place despite the virus's monthly death toll dropping. Whether it was social distancing measures, compulsory mask-wearing, curfews, tracking of individuals, or limitations of how many people could gather in one place, few if any of these restrictions had been lifted.

Which Emma found strange.

She clearly recalled the COVID-related regulations had initially been introduced by politicians as "temporary measures" to "flatten the curve" in order to "return to normal as quickly as possible." Somehow that had all morphed into "the new normal" which she feared might end up being a long-term system of tyranny.

Emma also feared that compulsory vaccinations involving rushed and poorly-tested vaccines would be next up. The introduction of compulsory microchips was another fear. She also sensed a technocratic future in which increasing censorship would eventually kill off free speech for good.

If she was being honest, though, she did not have any firm beliefs anymore about what the hell was going on. And she knew she wasn't alone. Friends, associates and even strangers had confided they felt much the same. Like a cork being tossed around in the ocean. That was how one friend had described his current state of mind, and she felt much the same.

The year, she thought, would be an amazing year to study in an academic way.

Like, if it were the year 2050 and we could research 2020 in a history class... But unfortunately we are living in it and have to figure this shit out in the here and now!

The year had completely screwed with her head and Emma certainly didn't feel as sure about everything as she had earlier in Wuhan. Since then her mom had almost died, which had meant Emma had come into the orbit of mortality for the first time in her life. She'd also just turned twenty, and somehow no longer being a teen was a reminder that she did not know as much about the world as she previously thought she did. Sure, she'd read a fair bit and debated a lot online and had tried to consider as many different philosophies as she could, but deep down she knew she still lacked life experience.

Conversely, she also felt like she'd matured a decade throughout the course of the year. And with that had come some humility. In hindsight, she realized it was a necessary dose of humility for she knew deep down the world was more complex than her teenage self had assumed.

Emma looked back at her mother who was still engaging with others on her video conference call out on the apartment balcony. Observing her standing there, alive and even looking reasonably healthy, she felt as if she was witnessing a miracle.

39

- --- --. . - .... . .-. .- .--. .- .-. -

QALANDIA, WEST BANK, PALESTINE

AT THE SAME time the conference call was taking place between Elijah and his followers, Mariam was staring at the face of a young Israeli soldier who looked to be no more than eighteen or nineteen. His features were slightly obscured by other Palestinians, but even from twenty feet away she could see he had severe acne on his cheeks and forehead. His pale skin accentuated his acne.

Mariam was queuing with Fadi and others at the Qalandia checkpoint, which was controlled by the Israel Defense Forces or IDF. There was little room to move as barbed wire fences and cages pressed in on either side of the queue.

Fadi tensed and held on tight to his mother's hand as an armed female IDF soldier walked slowly along the queue toward them. Barely older than her male comrade, the soldier carried the IDF's weapon of choice – a US-supplied M4 carbine. She looked suspiciously at each Palestinian she passed as she approached.

Neither Mariam nor Fadi had a clue whether it was a rifle or a machine gun she carried, but it momentarily mesmerized them both as sunlight reflected off its shiny, black, metallic surface and into their eyes. The soldier paid little attention to the pair as she passed by.

Mother and son had already passed through seven Israeli-run military checkpoints so far. This one, in the small West Bank town of Qalandia, was the final one they and their fellow Palestinians had to pass through before entering Jerusalem. No easy task considering it was the main military checkpoint.

Mariam was aware that beyond the checkpoint a bus was waiting to take her and Fadi into Israel – specifically to Ben Gurion International Airport in Tel Aviv. From there they would catch a flight to Rio de Janeiro, in Brazil, where Hanan would be waiting to meet them.

The Aida refugee was holding recently acquired passports issued by the Palestinian Authority, as well as Palestinian identity cards and medical certificates proving she and Fadi were COVID-free. Everything except the medical certificates had been organized for them by Hanan.

Mariam had never been anywhere beyond the Middle East. She'd never been on Israeli soil for that matter. All she'd ever known was the West Bank.

Something made her turn around. She spied a mural on a wall away in the distance, deep in Palestine. She did a doubletake when she noticed the mural depicted a huge key.

Fadi noticed his mother suddenly looked lost in her own thoughts. Concerned, he gently touched her shoulder. "What's wrong, mother? What are you thinking of?"

"A promise."

"What kind of promise?"

"A…very serious one…"

"When was this promise made?"

"A long time ago."

Still lost in thought, Mariam looked down at the reddish soil beneath her feet.

Seven-year-old Mariam scuffed her bare feet on the red earth of Palestine. It was the year 1991 and she was holding the hand of her grandfather Joseph.

Joseph was a tall, wise-looking, protestant minister now in his 70th year. The Christian clergyman had seen so much change in his lifetime that he still had trouble comprehending what had happened to his own family and to Palestinians in general.

Grandfather and granddaughter were in the small West Bank city of Qalqilya, having taken a rare excursion from Aida refugee camp. Qalqilya was many miles to the north of Aida and Bethlehem, the only places young Mariam had ever visited previously. She was unsure why her beloved grandfather had brought her to this particular location. No matter. She enjoyed being with him regardless.

Joseph looked around. He surveyed several buildings he remembered from his youth, but almost everything was different now. So different it made him cringe. Especially as Qalqilya was now completely surrounded by the Israeli West Bank wall. Everywhere he looked, he could see the hallmarks of Israeli military occupation with signs in Hebrew, army symbols, roadblocks and security posts.

Having been born in 1921, Joseph was among the last of his generation of Palestinians. He was among the few who could recall a time when this land was open to all people and without the divisiveness that existed now.

Joseph suddenly looked down at Mariam, his piercing brown eyes boring into hers. His all-knowing eyes, not to mention his height, used to make her nervous. Not now, though. Now she could feel the warmth emanating from him despite his towering presence.

Bending down as if about to share a secret, he said, "Mariam, do you know the significance of this place?"

The small girl looked around and shrugged her shoulders as she realized she had no idea what importance Qalqilya had.

"Before Zionism came to these lands, Christians, Jews and Muslims all lived peacefully together... Here and all over Palestine. We were all like brothers and sisters. One big community."

Joseph retrieved the backpack he carried on his back and from it he pulled out a pair of binoculars, which he placed the over granddaughter's eyes.

Looking through the binoculars, Mariam felt her grandfather gently guide her vision until she found herself looking past the Israeli West Bank wall. As Joseph adjusted the zoom setting on the binoculars, she found herself looking at a solitary house on the other side of the valley beyond the border wall. The old house had a red roof; a large barn could be seen on a field alongside it.

As the house was beyond the wall, Mariam was aware it was in the forbidden land called Israel, which was off limits to her, or anyone like her.

"Before the Nakba," Joseph said, "my family... your family... our ancestors... lived in that house for centuries. We farmed the land, and we ran other businesses, and we welcomed guests of all races and religions to stay in our house."

Mariam listened intently as she continued to view the house with the distinctive red roof. She loved the way her grandfather spoke to her as an adult. Not that she always understood everything he said.

Joseph continued, "Then one night, in 1948, the dogs of one of Ben Gurion's militia started barking. I remember it like it was yesterday. The Zionists ransacked our house. They took my father and imprisoned him, and we never saw him again. My brother and I hid in that barn you see there" – he adjusted the binoculars so that his granddaughter was looking at the barn – "and we gathered some weapons. But the militia had already killed others in our neighborhood and resistance was futile."

Without looking up, Mariam asked, "What happened, grandfather?"

"We and our neighbors were thrown out of our homes that very night. Within days we became people without a land and we were forcibly consigned to living in tents in refugee camps."

Joseph took the binoculars from Mariam and returned them to his backpack, which he slipped over his broad shoulders once more. He took his granddaughter by the hand again and led her over to a large wooden chair beneath a tree where he invited her to sit on his lap.

The old man looked at Mariam for several seconds before pulling a large, rusty, old key from his pocket. It was made of a metal she had ever seen before. She went to touch it, but Joseph kept it out of reach as if to protect it. "My mother, before she passed away in 1949, gave me this key," he said grimly. "It is the key to that very house." He pointed to the house Mariam had just been looking at.

Hanging on his every word, the little girl looked back at the house over in Israeli territory.

Joseph continued, "My mother told me her faith in Jesus Christ assured her that one day Zionism will collapse, and Palestine will be free once more. And so, she gave me that key to the house as my inheritance. My only inheritance. She made me promise her, and God, that I will remain here on this land until such time as this key can be used to open the door of our house again… Or if not that I would pass the key on to my descendants so they will do the honor of one day returning home."

Mariam looked at Joseph gravely as she slowly comprehended what was being asked of her.

"I am dying now, Mariam. Doctors tell me I may not even make it until Christmas. Your mother and her brothers do not have the same spirit that I see in your eyes. So, I need you to promise me... and promise God... that you will remain on Palestinian soil and put that key in the door of our family home one day."

Mariam jumped as she was jolted back to the present-day as an IDF soldier announced that Fadi and herself would have their papers checked next. Her gaze returned to the key on the distant Palestinian mural then she slowly looked around at Qalandia checkpoint once more.

The young woman noticed the barbed wire, the cages, the concrete walls, the guns, the barriers, and the myriad of other symbols of the Israeli occupation of her ancestors' land. It looked like hell on Earth where Palestinians, including children, were being pushed around and herded like sheep through the narrow, prison-like, caged corridor.

She clutched the bronze cross around her neck.

Jesus give me strength for what I am about to do.

She reached down into her trouser pocket, unzipped it and pulled out the large key her grandfather had given her. She held it high above her head all the while a bemused Fadi watched her. Smiling at him, she said "Fear not, my son."

Mariam turned her face to the sky. "Free Palestine!" she screamed defiantly. "Free Palestine!"

Fadi's eyes opened wide and IDF soldiers nearby clutched their weapons as if they were suddenly under attack.

Fadi turned to his mother in disbelief. "What are you doing, mother? You will ruin everything!"

"One day you will understand, Fadi," Mariam said, grabbing his hand. "We are not going anywhere today. I will not leave the land of our ancestors!" She led her confused son away from the inhumane military checkpoint, ignoring the bemused looks being directed her way by the soldiers and by those other Palestinians queuing up.

Mariam pulled out her cellphone and urgently tried to call Hanan but got no answer. She wasn't to know that Hanan had blocked incoming calls so she could give her undivided attention to Elijah and the others in the continuing video conference call.

Nor did Mariam know what she was going to do with Fadi. She hoped he could still get to Brazil one day soon.

Perhaps Hanan will adopt him so he can pursue his professional tennis ambitions.

Despite the uncertain future they both now faced, she felt strangely content. The memory of the promise she made her grandfather had reignited the flames of defiance in her, and she felt more alive than she had in some time.

She also had a renewed faith and was certain that one day, in the coming months or years, her Lord and Savior Jesus Christ would help Palestinians reclaim all their stolen lands. She didn't know whether it would be the result of a war or some other major event, but all she knew for sure was that it would happen.

For the second time in as many minutes, she turned her face to the sky.

This time, she didn't scream defiantly; this time, she murmured, "From the river to the sea, Palestine will be free."

40

- --- --. . - .... . .-. .- .--. .- .-. -

BALI, INDONESIA

"**Y**OU HAVE ALL transformed yourselves," Elijah said, "and I'm very proud of every one of you. You've begun to transmute the pain you've all experienced into wisdom."

Elijah looked away from his phone's screen to observe the sparkling, foam-flecked wave sets rolling in at Kuta Beach as he thought of something else. Specifically, he was picturing family members he'd soon be reunited with back in London.

"As for my year… I have finally healed a decade-long rift with Mark, my brother. And I am adopting my niece who I will look after with all the love I can muster."

The others on the call couldn't hide their surprise upon learning that their spiritual teacher had been navigating his own personal issues during the year while also teaching them. Those others were Heather, Albert, Levi and Hanan, and this was a continuation of the same video meeting they'd been on for over an hour already.

Elijah closed his eyes as if to tune in and receive inner guidance. He wondered whether in years to come, with the benefit of hindsight, humanity would view all the radical events of 2020 as game-changing moments in history.

Will this year eventually end up being viewed as some kind of new beginning?

Or else the beginning of The End?

And so, are we now heading to an Apocalypse or will the world survive?

If humanity does survive are we going to have a dystopian or utopian civilization?

Or might there be some kind of split in humanity from now on, like a bifurcation point, where utopian and dystopian communities will both co-exist on the planet?

As he tuned in further, Elijah began to consider more esoteric possibilities.

Could certain quantum physics concepts be valid in this scenario, whereby there are infinite possible futures?

Is it a case where every person is actually a universe unto themselves, even though it seems as if we are all like ants living in a world that operates independently of us?

Are we all actually projecting the illusion of the world from our own personal consciousness?

Could it therefore be possible that some people who select fear will end up experiencing an Armageddon, while others who select love will experience a world that becomes heaven on Earth?

Elijah didn't have any clear answers, only questions. His mind drifted to the future as he considered whether or not the world would ever return to normal.

And what about 2021? Will that be more of the same or will it be more reflective of 2019 and earlier years in recent history?

When will regular human interactions, such as children freely playing or big gatherings without social distancing, resume?

He opened his eyes again, returning his attention to the four spiritual seekers sharing the video conference call with him.

"So as the end of 2020 nears, we find ourselves diving deep in the universe's infinite waters... "

Elijah looked at every one of his seekers on the screen.

"There's a quote by Charles Dickens from *A Tale of Two Cities*, which I believe speaks to this moment in time we find ourselves in..."

He could see he had the undivided attention of the group. Hanan was now driving home in Rio, Levi was standing in a boarding queue inside Sydney International Airport's departure terminal, Heather was cooking in the kitchen of her Houston apartment while Albert was still sitting outside the café overlooking Lake Zürich.

"It was the best of times, it was the worst of times, it was the age of wisdom, it was the age of foolishness, it was the epoch of belief, it was the epoch of incredulity, it was the season of light, it was the season of darkness, it was the spring of hope, it was the winter of despair."

Elijah smiled at his followers. He was finally receiving some clarity about the year that was coming to a close – and he just hoped his followers were having personal epiphanies as well.

"So maybe the lesson here with the global pandemic and economic meltdown and talk of the apocalypse, is that we needed to experience darkness. We must love the darkness and the light. That is the totality of ourselves for we are duality. And we can only ever heal if we understand all aspects of ourselves, and all aspects of the world... And you have all shown the necessary courage to deny nothing, to accept the light and the darkness. For that's the only way we can ever become whole."

Elijah, who remained in the lotus position, noticed a large, blue butterfly flying around his head. It settled on his knee. He reached out to touch the butterfly and *she* – for that was how he thought of her – actually let him stroke her wings. The butterfly then moved slowly into the palm of his hand.

The Englishman knew that butterflies were symbolic of various deep and meaningful concepts. A Thai Buddhist teacher had once told him that arrival of butterflies in general, of any color or species, was life indicating change or rebirth was occurring. The teacher had also told him that blue butterflies were a symbol of love.

Elijah remembered reading that the appearance of a blue butterfly was also a sign of good fortune being just around the corner. However, as he continued to study the brilliant blue creature in his palm he asked himself what her appearance meant to him. To him personally.

After a few moments it occurred to him that the bright blue color shining off the butterfly somehow represented the interconnectedness of everything. And that all the recent positive changes he'd made in his life were perhaps not totally separate from the improvements Heather, Albert, Levi and Hanan had made in their own lives.

Together, simultaneously, we all realigned with our true natures.

Elijah watched as the butterfly flew out of his hand and allowed herself to be carried further along the shoreline by the gentle sea breeze.

THE END

If you liked this story, the author would greatly appreciate a review from you on Amazon.

Other book titles by James Morcan follow over page…

OTHER BOOKS BY JAMES MORCAN
(CO-WRITTEN WITH LANCE MORCAN)
AND PUBLISHED BY STERLING GATE BOOKS

CONSPIRACY THRILLERS:

The Ninth Orphan (The Orphan Trilogy, #1)

The Orphan Factory (The Orphan Trilogy, #2)

The Orphan Uprising (The Orphan Trilogy, #3)

SUSPENSE THRILLERS:

Silent Fear

The Me Too Girl

The Heathrow Affair

ACTION-ADVENTURE:

High Country Contract:

The Dogon Initiative (The Deniables, Book 1)

HISTORICAL FICTION:

White Spirit (A novel based on a true story)

Into the Americas (A novel based on a true story)

World Odyssey (The World Duology, #1)

Fiji: A Novel (The World Duology, #2)

NON-FICTION:

Debunking Holocaust Denial Theories

The Orphan Conspiracies:
29 Conspiracy Theories from the Orphan Trilogy

Genius Intelligence:
Secret Techniques and Technologies to Increase IQ
(The Underground Knowledge Series, #1)

Antigravity Propulsion:
Human or Alien Technologies?
(The Underground Knowledge Series, #2)

Medical Industrial Complex:
The $ickness Industry, Big Pharma and Suppressed Cures
(The Underground Knowledge Series, #3)

The Catcher In The Rye Enigma:
J.D. Salinger's Mind Control Triggering Device or a
Coincidental Literary Obsession of Criminals?
(The Underground Knowledge Series, #4)

International Bankster$:
The Global Banking Elite Exposed and the Case for
Restructuring Capitalism
(The Underground Knowledge Series, #5)

Bankrupting The Third World:
How the Global Elite Drown Poor Nations in a Sea of Debt
(The Underground Knowledge Series, #6)

Underground Bases:
Subterranean Military Facilities and the Cities Beneath Our Feet
(The Underground Knowledge Series, #7)

Vaccine Science Revisited:
Are Childhood Immunizations as Safe as Claimed?
(The Underground Knowledge Series, #8)